THE EARTH ACCORDING TO GIDEON

ROAD TRIPS IN SPACE SERIES, BOOK 2

CRAIG ROBERTSON

IMAGINE-IT PUBLISHING

CONTENTS

THE EARTH ACCORDING TO GIDEON

ROAD TRIPS IN SPACE SERIES, BOOK 2

By Craig Robertson

The Earth Must Have Been a Bad Planet In a Former Lifetime. Gideon's Coming...

Imagine-It Publishing
El Dorado Hills, CA

ALSO BY CRAIG ROBERTSON:

BOOKS IN THE RYANVERSE:

THE FOREVER SERIES (2016)

THE FOREVER LIFE, Book 1

THE FOREVER ENEMY, Book 2

THE FOREVER FIGHT, Book 3

THE FOREVER QUEST, Book 4

THE FOREVER ALLIANCE, Book 5

THE FOREVER PEACE, Book 6

GALAXY ON FIRE SERIES (2017)

EMBERS, Book 1

FLAMES, Book 2

FIRESTRORM, Book 3

FIRES OF HELL, Book 4

DRAGON FIRE, Book 5

ASHES, Book 6

RISE OF ANCIENT GODS SERIES (2018):

RETURN OF THE ANCIENT GODS, Book 1

RAGE OF THE ANCIENT GODS, Book 2

TORMENT OF THE ANCIENT GODS, Book 3

WRATH OF THE ANCIENT GODS, Book 4

FURY OF THE ANCIENT GODS, Book 5

FALL OF THE ANCIENT GODS, Book 6

TIME WARS LAST FOREVER SERIES (2019)

RYAN TIME, Book 1

LOST TIME, BOOK 2

NON-RYANVERSE BOOKS:

ROAD TRIPS IN SPACE SERIES (2019):

THE GALAXY ACCORDING TO GIDEON, Book 1

THE EARTH ACCORDING TO GIDEON, Book 2

STANDALONE WORKS:

THE CORPORATE VIRUS (2016)

TIME DIVING (2013)

THE INNERgLOW EFFECT (2010)

WRITE NOW! THE PRISONER OF NaNoWRiMo (2009)

ANON TIME (2009)

ISBN: 978-1-7331137-8-6 (Print)
978-1-7331137-7-9(E-Book)

Cover design by Alexandre
http://www.designbookcover.pt/en/

Editing by Michael R. Blanche

Formatting by Drew Avera
www.drewavera.com/book-formatting

Editing reading help by Charlie "The Bagpiper" Pitts

First Edition 2019

No series of mine would be proper or complete without a dedication to my beautiful bride, my love, my wife ... my Karen.

PRELUDE

Swobo Grabski sat in his cubical and radiated anger. He was positively incandescent with rage. Swobo had known true, pure, unadulterated love, but it was stolen away from him. Well, it was, *technically*, adulterated love, since he was married the entire time. That factoid did not, however, detract from the ecstasy he had held so close to his bosom. He had known *minutes* of unblemished love, several times during the period his precious was his. And, even after her .. er, *unfortunate* change, Swobo had known many consecutive minutes of rapture, allbethey more cautious interactions, where he had to substitute a modicum of vigilance for passionate abandon. But they were good minutes, in his otherwise sentence of a life.

As an assistant to an associate accountant's handler, his world was one long tunnel of darkness. Being married to Battle-Axe all those long, seemingly endless years, did nothing to lighten his burden of despair. That he ignored the red flashing lights and blaring horns of warning and wed a female named Battle-Axe was, upon reflection, unwise. You might wonder what degenerate form of parent would name their infant girl *Battle-Axe*. They were prescient, that's what they were. For, with their first glance at the crusty, wailing thing, they knew they'd made a mistake for which they would—and should—be held accountable.

But, *his precious* had been the pin-prick of starlight, piercing the blackness that was the midnight sky of Swobo's crushingly inadequate life. And the scoundrel, that horrible, horrible man, had taken his adulterated lover away. As Swobo Grabski sat there, hour upon interminable hour, in his cubicle, assisting the handler of an associate accountant, which was a bleak career, to say the very least, all he could focus on was *revenge*. Cold, cruel, and oh-so-sweet revenge. Swobo Grabski was nothing more than a turd being flushed down life's cruel passageway, of that he was certain. He was equally certain that he was going to kill the man who had ruined his only succor, his intimate services consultant, his abiding love, Hephzibah ...uh... whatever her last name might have been.

There was no doubt, whatsoever, that Gideon Prime would die. Horrifically, painfully, and, if possible, repeatedly. Swobo Grabski would not be made a fool of. At least, not more than he already was, completely and utterly, by every force of nature and individual he'd ever   had   an   interaction   with.

CHAPTER ONE

"No, no, kiddo. You hold it like this," Gideon said, encouragingly.

"I think I know how to hold one of these. Trust me, I've had *lots* of experience." She snickered quietly. "Even when they're this small."

"That's not funny, and, in fact, I do believe it's hurtful," protested Gideon. "A man has both pride in, and no control over, how big, or not big (never say small in this reference), these things are."

"Oh, I am *sorely* aware of that," she guffawed. "If a girl doesn't say it's the biggest she's ever seen, the entire experience is out the window. So might be any tip, also."

"Well, er, I think it's not *too* small," observed an uncertain Rigel. "And size doesn't matter as much as they say it does. It's really all about the taste."

"Said someone who has never gotten even *this* lucky," mocked Gideon.

"Rigel, dear," began Zebah, "must you stare? It makes this all the harder."

"Harder?" snapped Gideon. "If this got any harder, someone'd receive a nasty cut."

Zebah snickered through her nose so hard, a trickle of snot came out.

"That's it," shouted Gideon, in frustration. "Give me back my fish. I'll fillet it myself."

"Not hardly," teased Zebah. "You can't separate meat from the bone when they're that tiny. One slice, and you'll make mush out of it."

"Mushy sushi," said Rigel, with a nasal chuckle.

"It's official," pronounced Gideon. "I'm done with fishing. With you two along, it's my childhood, all over again. Gideon, you're too small. Gideon, you can't do anything right. Gideon, put the pin back in and *then* hand me the grenade." He stood and wiped his hands on Rigel's shirt.

"Hey, don't get that on me," yelped Rigel.

"What about this poor fish?" Zebah asked, pointing down toward it.

"Not my problem." He pointed at the fish. "It's *his* problem, not mine."

"Hey, jocko," the carnie shouted at Gideon. "You still owe me two tokens for dat fish."

"It's not my fish," Gideon replied. "You can do a DNA test, if you like. I never saw that fish before in my life."

"You threw the ping-pong ball into the cute, if outdated, glass container. Ergo, *dat's* your fish and you owe me two tokens." The fellow held out two of his furry hands to receive payment. It was hard to say which appendage was the filthiest, though in reality, that didn't actually matter. What they all were was empty of tokens.

Gideon patted his various pockets. "I seem to be temporarily out of tokens. I'm certain I had quite a few. Wait," he exclaimed turning to address Zebah, "isn't this the pair of trousers with the holes in the pockets?"

She grinned. "Beats me."

"Da little lady's tinking pretty much what I am. Beats *you,*" threatened the Perplexian carnival attendant.

"Oh, that's bad," said Gideon, with a very serious tone. "Your remark was neither witty, nor did it follow from my sister's idiomatic phrasing. Here's what I *will* do. You take a second. Formulate a cogent, credible verbal threat, one that'll really have this fellow quaking in his boots." Gideon set a hand on Rigel's shoulder. "If you come up with a winner, you can perform the act on him, and I won't stand in your way. Hmm? How's that sound?"

"My beef's wit you, ugly puss, not your lover boy, dar." the Perplexian smiled evilly, with both his mouths.

Gideon glanced to the right, then, suspiciously to the left. Conspiratorially, he leaned into the purveyor of carnival game entertainment. "What's your name, friend?"

"No, I'm not."

"Well, Noimnot, look at it this way." Gideon relooked to both sides, suspiciously. "I never *had* any money." He gestured to Zebah. "She never *had* any money." He turned his harshest of stares to Rigel. "This man, on the other hand, had a *boatload*. When I told him I wanted to win my dying sister, here, a fish, to possibly take with her to the grave, he said he'd spot me the cash."

Gideon jumped, and spun, like an electric eel had zapped him from behind. One hadn't.

The attendant's head darted, in sympathy with how, if not comprehending why, Gideon's body had so contorted.

"But, noooo. My cousin, Bingo, here," Gideon nodded toward Rigel, "just had to have one of those warm, sweet, dripping with goodness funnel cakes, over there." Gideon bobbed his head repeatedly at the greasy food vendor, just across the wide isle. "You see them? I especially like the ones with so much whipped cream slathered over them that you can't even see the luscious, warm, fruit mixture hiding, just for you to enjoy, under its fluffy surface."

Gideon got a lascivious look on his face, and stared at Zebah, lustfully. "Did you read that recent report in the medical journal?"

The Perplexian, who actually did have a name, but it didn't matter, shrugged. "I guess not."

"Medical science has just *proven* that funnel cakes with excess whipped cream and too much warm, calorie-laden fruit compote are ..." He rechecked left, right, and left, again. No one was there. "Are unstoppable aphrodisiacs?" He rocketed his eyebrows and repeatedly elbowed the carny.

"You don't say?" he replied with a hot lungful of air.

Gideon, in near panic, placed his finger over his lips. "Shhhuusshhh. Geez. You want everyone to hear you? Imagine what the line'd do then?" Gideon, always a helper, pointed to the line of two people, queued up for funnel cakes. "You know, the article just came out ten minutes ago. Look," he pounded a finger in the direction of the elderly couple, waiting to make yet another poor food decision in their long life together studded with poor food choices.

"They clearly read the article. Why, in minutes, the line will be so long ... so ... I ... I can't even bring myself to say the words." Gideon hid his eyes in the crook of his elbow. He seemed unable to soldier on.

The carny gently but decidedly placed a hand on Gideon's shoulder. "What, pal. What will the line be so long dat you can't even say da words concerning?"

Gideon was finally able to look back on the elderly couple. He sniffed, loudly. "They'll run out of funnel cakes."

As if learning his wife and children had just been swallowed by a whale, the carny gasped, "No."

Gideon could only nod in the affirmative. But, he finally found the resolve to say, "And you, working so hard here, at this wonderful stand, will not be able to purchase the most vroom-vroom aphrodisiac ever discovered, that additionally taste like you died and went to Heaven."

"Are ... are you certain, pal?"

Gideon nodded, tragically.

Then, a wavelet of hope crossed Gideon's darkened countenance. "Wait." Again he check left, right, left. "There is one chance, one crazy chance."

"*What*," he responded as he shook Gideon.

"If it's alright with me, you could go over, secure a place in line, and purchase several of those divine gifts from God."

11

"If it's okay with you?"

"If it's okay with," he hugged Zebah and Rigel, "*us*."

"Oooh, come on. You guys gotta say *yes*. Please, can I go get in line before there is no hope of resurrecting my sex life, which currently can only be characterized as in shambles?" He was tearful and distraught.

Gideon was barely able to raise a glance to his companions. They looked—well, *stupefied* might be one description.

"They say that we can say *yes*," Gideon triumphed. He set a hand on the burly fellow's shoulder and shoved him away. Waving warmly, he called after the Perplexian, "We'll watch the attraction while you save your marriage, your life, and your very fut ..."

The second the carny was out of earshot, Gideon shouted, "Rigel, clean out the cash box."

"Me," he protested. "why don't *you* clean out the cash box.

"Busy,"   he   huffed.   "I'm   in   it   for   the   fishes."

CHAPTER TWO

The three travelers sat at a budget-oriented drinking establishment on the outskirts of Peoria, Illinois, called Sticky's. It was, as an aside, unclear if the bar was so named because the owner, Red Dresser, was so thin, or because every surface in the dive was, you got it, sticky. Sticky's was located between Peoria's only all-amateur strip club, and Brother Bert's Rescue Mission and Taxidermy. Hence, business was sparse during the best of times. Rigel, Zebah, and Gideon were the lone celebrants in the bar, unless one counted the two figures in the corner. It was unclear if they were recent visitors from the strip club, and in stunned silence based on the horrors they witnessed, or if they were on loan from the taxidermy next door. Either way, it was difficult to count them as being actively present.

Rigel counted, for the fifth time, the take from the carny's cash box. Gideon was transfixed with the transferring of small goldfish from one container to the another. Zebah was so bored she was considering propositioning the two stiffs—the ones that *weren't* Rigel and Gideon, that is. The side of her face rested in a palm, and she had the distant look of someone recently deflated as her only expression.

"You said we'd come to Earth and it would be fun, fun, and more fun," Zebah said, though she was somewhat hard to understand, with her mouth partly pressed firmly against her hand.

Without looking up, Gideon held a finger up to her. "Ah, ah. I said we were going to Earth. I never said anything about fun, fun, unbridled fun."

She sat up. "Then why'd we come here?" she questioned indignantly.

He held out his hand to her. "Hi, my name's Gideon Prime."

She rolled her eyes. "You came here to scam. You came here to get something for nothing. You came here to get rich quick, and split."

He waggled his eyebrows. "I can tell we've met."

"Seriously, Gideon? You actually think we can get rich quick on this regressive rock?"

"Absolutely. We're the only game in town. How can we *not* get rich quick?"

"Well, since you ask, here's your first clue. There's a big galaxy out there, and we're the only game in town. If there was money to be made, don't you think the place'd be crawling with con men?"

"There has to be a first time for every great undertaking. This place is ripe for the picking. Trust me, I got instincts."

Rigel smiled like he'd won a beauty contest, and held his arms out to their recent take. "Fifty-seven dollars and thirteen cents. Not bad, for a start, I'd say."

"How are we ever going to spend that much money?" she mocked.

"I *know*," squealed Rigel.

"Look," she said with disgust, "that's not even chump change. Hell, it would barely cover our bill, if we were actually going to pay it."

Gideon gestured to her harshly. "*Watch* your mouth, young lady. I will not have that kind of language in my presence. *Pay the bill.* Honestly, the type of obscenity you are capable of broadcasting is getting worse by the day."

"Okay, fearless leader," she challenged, "what's our plan, this time? How are we going to build on our fifty-seven dollars and thirteen cents?"

"Slowly, at first, then, as we take on momentum, faster and faster. We'll be rich before you know it."

Rigel looked up from his seventh recount. "How will we know we're rich before we know we're rich? Wouldn't we have to know, to know?"

"Move on, pal. You're getting bogged down by the details, yet again. Think *big*."

"*Gideon*," Zebah said with all the knowing frustration the universe had to offer, "you're doing it again." She passed a hand in the direction of the fifty-seven dollars and thirteen cents. "We're broke, you're dreaming, and I'm thinking of getting a legit job because I'm so damn over this."

Gideon paled alarmingly. "Le—" He stopped to gain strength. Closing his eyes, and swallowing, hard, he tried to rally. "Leg ... leggg ... honest work? Babe, how could you even think those words, let alone subject me to hearing them?"

She rolled her eyes. "It's always all about you, isn't it?"

Her stared at her, waiting for her to continue to some conversational point.

"You're not responding," she observed with displeasure.

"You never finished your speaking thing," he protested.

"I most certainly did. I said it's all about you."

He rolled his hands in the air between them, inviting her to continue.

"What?" she snapped.

"It's all about me, and..."

"And nothing. That's the problem. It's all about you in your head."

"Of course it is. What's your point? I'm assuming you have one."

"Forget it."

"Already have," he replied truthfully.

"If I might," began Rigel, tentatively. "I believe what Zebah's saying is we're in an all-too-familiar situation. Broke, no prospects, and, well, broke. A change, such as our being rich, overflowing with prospects, and, well, rich, would be an agreeable change."

"Do you recall those Rock-Like Mountains we crossed, getting here?" Gideon asked, winding up to be inspirational.

They both cringed, as they knew it was coming.

"You mean the *Rocky* Mountains?" asked Zebah, dubiously.

"Thank you for confirming that's what I said."

Rather than fight a losing battle, she let it pass.

"When we crossed those pious peaks, do you recall what we saw, covering those precarious precipices?"

"I couldn't see anything," Rigel mused pathetically. "I was on the floor, looking down, with you two sitting on my back."

"*Duh*," returned Gideon. "Those boxcars don't exactly have comfy seats. Where was this tender vision *going* to sit, if not on something cushiony?"

"Guys, we're drifting off point," Zebah snapped.

"We saw lots of mighty trees, rising majestically to the heavens."

He looked to his companions.

Cue the crickets.

"The trees. They began from tiny seeds." He slid the pittance of cash toward himself. "This tiny seed will grow into a majestic money tree. You'll see."

Cue more crickets, larger ones.

"No, it won't, fool," stated Zebah, dispassionately. "You will bet it, blow it, or otherwise abuse that money. You always do. What do we do then? Where are we going to get real, *actual* funding?"

Funding. That version of incoming spendable money rang a distant bell in Gideon's generally empty head. Funding. Where had he heard that ...

"*I got it*," he declared, boldly. "We are going where cash comes from. Where it *flows* from. Where cash money is the coin of the realm."

"Where *money* is the *coin* of the realm?" That was Zebah. She was more astounded than usual. "Where *isn't* money the coin of the realm?"

"I give up? Where?" he replied, innocently.

She balled up her hands, arms, and torso, condensing in a tight heap before his eyes.

"Charades? Babe, I got no time. We need to be somewhere, *soon* ... before we get old and don't care."

Zebah might have said, "Go on." It was hard to determine, given her tense contortion.

"Honey," he began.

"Me?" asked Rigel, tapping his chest.

"Why not? Honeys, we're going to the center of power, and, hence money. We're going to Washington."

"*Washington*," declared Rigel with an enormous smile. "What a capital idea. He'll surely lend us some money. I heard that, up until his death several centuries ago, he was a kind and generous man."

"We're not going to a dead guy, *again*?" Zebah expressed with consternation. "That never ends well."

She had a point.

"No, team. We're going to Washington, D.C."

Both Zebah and Rigel shot up an eyebrow.

"Seriously. It's where the money is."

Their eyebrows slackened. The man was right.

"The only real question is, what are we waiting for?"

"It's a long walk?" responded Rigel.

"This guy doesn't *walk* into Washington, D.C.," Gideon thumbed his chest.

"I don't think my back can take another train ride," whined Rigel.

"No. We're taking our ship."

"Our space craft ship?" Zebah said, darkly. "We're landing a UFO in the most powerful nation's capital?"

"Yes, we are," he responded, cheerily.

"Isn't that insane, suicidal, and absolutely foolhardy?"

"Only," he raised a finger, "if it backfires."

17

Slowly, one at a time, the travelers turned to see Red Dresser, the proprietor of Sticky's, standing mortician-like, at table side.

"May we help you, good inn keeper?" asked an irritated Gideon.

"Funny you should put it in those words, pal. As a matter of fact, the answer is *yes*. You *may*. You *may* pay your bill."

"*That* is a true statement, barkeep," responded a deadly serious Gideon. "We may. We may not. What's your purpose here, and, more critically, your point?"

"I've seen a million losers sit here and dream up yet another impossible scheme."

Gideon rested his chin on his palm. "You have? Fascinating. I'm, I'm speechless. You may go now. While you're gone, please do not return."

"More than happy. It's my goal, in this interaction, as it were. So," he nodded to the fifty-seven dollars and thirteen cents, "you pony up a bit more scratch, and then you leave. That way, I'm able to avoid the necessity of beating the ever living sh—"

The door of Sticky's opened and closed, noisily. It always did, since it was in such a state of disrepair. Three sets of eyes, all but Gideon's, checked out the newest arrival. Gideon didn't for two reasons. One, he couldn't possibly care who entered a dive bar. That would be silly. Two, he was already preoccupied pouring goldfish from a few bowls, into separate ones, to waste time looking elsewhere. He wanted, more than anything, to be a good pet owner.

"Ah, Gideon," Zebah began with fear and trepidation in her tone. "I think there's someone here to see you."

"That's nice," he replied, absently.

"*Not* necessarily," she opined.

"That's nice. Why do you think he's here to see me?"

"Ah, dude's got a crazed look in his eyes," she said, her concern apparent in her voice.

Gideon looked up, then quickly back down. "Nah. Could be here for any reason."

"He's heading right this way with singular focus."

Gideon looked up, then quickly back down. "Nah. Could be asking Red, here, for work."

"He *really* looks pissed," she said, panic creeping into her tone.

Gideon looked up, then quickly back down. "Nah. Could be here to try the mountain oyster and escargot sandwich."

"He's raising a very large machete into the air."

"Ah," Gideon said looking up, and not back down. "He is here to see me."

All eyes, this time, looked to see Swobo Grabski pounding his way to close the distance between himself, and sweet revenge. He stopped at the edge of the table, raised his weapon even higher, and aimed it at Gideon's forehead. And then he froze. At that increased angle, he could plainly see the apple of his devotion was, also, present.

"Hephzibah?" he said, melting. "Can it be you, love?"

She scowled. She knew this drill, all too well. Happened *all* the time with the crazies. "Have we met, punk?"

"Ha ... havvvv ... have we m ... mmm ... met?"

Oh, yeah. A crazy.

"You're my one true love. The one this *fiend* stole from me, thus ruining my already ruined life."

She allowed the philosophical aspects of his words pass, in the interest of time. "I repeat. Have we met?"

"Why, yes, devotion. You were my intimate services consultant, back on Opcurelon."

She twisted her mouth. "Private or group sessions?"

"Pri ... you gave group lessons?" The man was astounded.

"Every other Tuesday, and twice on Sundays."

"*Group* intimate services consultant sessions?" He was aghast.

"Some can't *afford* the private ones. Others," she looked disapprovingly at Gideon, "seem to *favor* the group activities."

"But I thought you loved me?"

"Then, you thought wrong." My, she'd learned to deliver that line like a matador does a sword.

"But, even after ... you know, your issue, I was a loyal student."

"You mean when I was a zombie?" she howled in disgust. "That seals it, pallo. You're sick. Please leave."

Swobo Grabski began to grow both suspicious, and angry. "Or what?"

"Or what? I'll tell Gideon, and he'll deal with you, but good."

Gideon grinned, on the inside. He loved this part the best.

"Oh, you will, will you?" driveled Swobo Grabski. "I'll deal with *him*." He raised the machete, higher.

"Why are you aiming that at this man," Zebah indicated Gideon, "an innocent bystander?"

"He's not innocent. He is guilt. He's Gideon Prime and he must die."

"Be that as it may, *this* man's not Gideon Prime." She pointed directly at Gideon Prime.

"Yes, he is, isn't he?" responded a confused would-be assassin.

"*This* man is Gideon Prime," she declared, switching her finger to identify Red Dresser.

"Are you *sure*?" wheezed Swobo Grabski.

"Are you *sure*?" wheezed Red Dresser.

"The man's my pimp. I think I know who the man who forces me into performing all forms of sordid sex acts, the one who keeps me from being with my one true love, *is*, don't I?" Pro that she was, she iced the cake by kissing the air in his direction, with her, puffy, ruby red lips.

Bingo!

Swobo Grabski realigned his blade at Red's head.

20

Catching on, slowly, Red raised his arms. "Now wait ... ahhhhhh—"

Swobo Grabski did not offer the man who'd crushed his dreams to speak *one more lie*, before he was dismembered.

Red, no stranger to *this* drill, bolted.

Swobo Grabski, a greater fool than one would have presupposed he could possibly be, followed, screaming and spitting, lost to his blood lust.

The three travelers watched the spectacle depart.

"Where was I?" asked Gideon, sounding rather bored.

"Washington, *DC*, not the corpse," responded Rigel.

"Ah yes. Washington, District of Cash."

At   least   he   had   that   part   right.

CHAPTER THREE

After landing their Jump Back A-11-2b Star Vagabond on the South Lawn of the White House, our trio emerged, and waited impatiently for what they assumed would be great commotion and fanfare. After thirty minutes of ongoing anonymity, Gideon was done.

"Come on," he said in snit, "let's get this show on the road."

The others followed, quietly. They breezed into the Visitor's Entrance without an issue. Some screening persons had asked for ID and that they pass through some sort of cleansing unit, but they deferred. Gideon used his hand brain-scrubber to weasel them in, unclean, or whatever. And, for any patriotic, caring readers, please know that very few National Park Service personnel were damaged in the process, and none seriously so.

They strolled through the East Wing, finding it positively useless, with its assembly halls, library, and flower shop. Seriously. What would they buy flowers for? None were edible. They took the stairs to the next floor up, after only minor interaction with obstructive employees. But, again, the space was useless. Colored rooms, blue, red, and the poorest excuse for green any of them had seen. So, it was on to what one guard referred to as the West Wing, just before they reset his brain to a second grade level. Not to worry. The effect was transient. The working stiff'd be back at his post, hating each day there as much as he hated either of his former wives, or his supervisor, one of whom was one of the exes. Long story— and not actually important. Forget about the guard.

As they entered the West Wing, they were met by a stern looking woman in her middle years. She was seated behind a mahogany desk, scribbling. She did not seem, to the outsiders, to be reveling in her middle years, and she dressed as if she loathed herself. Upon hearing their approach, she set down her pen and folded her hands, tightly. Everything about the woman, in fact, looked to be wound way too tight. Rigel was emotionally and physically drawn to her, in a heartbeat.

"May I help you?" she said, unmistakable doubt filling her tone.

"Well, actually, sweetie, it would be super if you could," said Gideon, putting on his best warm-the-frigid-bitch's-heart smile. It deserves mention that he was *oh*-so-good at that one.

"I *beg* your pardon. I am not sweetie, *yours* or *anyone* else's." She looked, if it were possible, more stern and unyielding.

"Pity, that," he responded sadly, "but, no time to fix that, just now. You keep bearing that cross. Something good's gotta come your way, maybe."

Rigel started to say that he was more than willing to help, but Gideon was glaring at him to shut up, even before his lips parted. Gideon knew men's desires and guessed at Rigel's based on his being so pathetic.

"Ah, look, kind of in a rush, here," Gideon got down to it. "We're aliens. We want you to—" he snapped his fingers impatiently at Zebah.

"Take us to your leader," she finished his thought.

"Yeah, what the babe said."

"Sir, I do not know who you think you are—"

He interrupted the receptionist by shoving his hand just shy of her nose. "Gideon Prime, and yes, you are pleased to met me. Thanks."

"Remove that hand, or I will *have* it removed."

Gideon believed her, and withdrew his greeting.

"You say you are aliens?"

"Yes. Extremely alien." Gideon placed his thumbs in his ears and wagged his fingers in the air, while gyrating from side-to-side.

"I'm afraid you're in the incorrect federal facility. You want The United States Immigration and Naturalization Service. They are not located here. Please go to their offices. They will," she raised the back of her hand to cover her lips, and snickered something awful. "they will ... help—" more snickering, louder this time, "*help* you with your issues."

"You don't sound very confident in their abilities to address the needs of aliens," remarked Rigel, respectfully. Actually, he was simply hoping to start up an ice breaking conversation with the woman he'd fallen so completely in love with.

More snickering, bordering on outright laughter. Then, "No, sir. Sorry if you get that impression. They are *professionals*."

"Well, that's not what we're looking for, sweetie, We're *alien* aliens." He pointed over a shoulder. "Didn't you notice our UFO on the lawn, out there?"

"The object on the South Lawn is *your* space craft?"

"Yes, indeedy do," he replied, happy to be making headway, finally.

"Sir, it is not generally my place to point such issues out, but, in this case, I shall make an exception."

Oh, how Rigel wanted to have her babies. Or, was it the other way around?

"If the object on the South Lawn *is* your vehicle, it cannot be a UFO. It is, by your own admission, *identified* as yours, is it not?"

"Well, technically. But, in a very *real* sense, it is a UFO," Gideon defended.

Her face pruned up more, if such a thing were possible, by way of response.

Rigel was ready to vault the table and make her *his*. Or was it the other way around?

"Okay, okay, it's a late model, domestic minivan. There. Issue off the table. Now, we need to see your—" again he snapped his fingers loudly at Zebah.

"Your ruling love god."

"Your ruling love god," he repeated inattentively.

24

Zebah could, at times, really wind up Gideon. It was her greatest pleasure, in fact.

That was about it. Francis Jane Merryweather reached over to press the panic button.

Francis Jane Merryweather looked up to see three potentially stray visitors approaching her duty station. They were unfamiliar to her. She hated unfamiliar. It was, by definition, out of the ordinary and hence, unwelcome. It was ... vile.

"May I help you?" she said, unmistakable doubt filling her tone.

"Well, actually, sweetie, it would be super if you could," said Gideon, putting on his best let's-try-this-again-bitch smile. It deserves mention that he was *oh*-so-good at that one, also.

"I *beg* your pardon. I am not sweetie, *yours* or *anyone* else's." She looked, if it were possible, more stern and unyielding.

"Awe, come now," Gideon teased. "Then who's ring is that on the digitus annularis of your left hand?"

She started to berate the two-bit bumbler, but she did so by pointing at him with her left index finger. That is how she came to notice the wedding ring she sported, on the middle finger the guest had mentioned. "What the devil?" she squeaked. "How did that get there?"

Rigel cleared his throat, then rocked nervously on his heels. He looked away, and whistled, softly.

"You're asking *us*, sweetie?" Gideon pressed. "You don't have a drug or alcohol," he made air-quotation marks, "'*issue'*, do you?"

"I most certainly do not. Now, I'm going to get to the bottom of this, immediately." Francis Jane Merryweather reached over to press the panic button.

Francis Jane Merryweather looked up to see three potentially stray visitors approaching her duty station. They were unfamiliar to her. She hated unfamiliar. It was, by definition, out of the ordinary and hence, unwelcome. It was ... v ... v ... villainous? No, she shook her head clear, it was bile. *Vile*.

"May I help—" she began to say, when she noticed, for the first time ever, a picture of her, holding her infant child. She was, up to that point in time, unaware she *had* an infant child, but, a mother just knows.

"May I help you?" Gideon asked, in a most friendly manner.

"Mis ... umpostunan frumpl," she replied.

"Sorry. Are you Swedish?"

She shrugged to say she had no idea if she was Swedish or not.

"Look, kind of pressed for time, here. We have an appointment with the boss woman," Gideon pointed past Francis Jane Merryweather, down the hall.

"Fixilfizle," was all the new mom could muster.

"I'll stay behind," Rigel said, "if it's okay with you two?"

"You stay with the happy little family, Rige," beamed Gideon. "We'll snag you on the rebound."

Rigel grinned, stupidly.

"Getting to this Egg Office is harder than it should be," Gideon declared, as they cleared the next set of impediments.

"*Oval*, dear," corrected Zebah.

"Not now, hon. Time and place. Remember, we talked about this recently. Naughty sex is fun, but time *and* place." He tapped the side of his nose at her.

"Idiot," she hissed. "I meant it's the *Oval* Office, not the *Egg* Office?"

He stopped and turned to her. "Are you certain?"

"Absolutely."

"I rather prefer Egg, myself. You know," he expanded his hands away from his head, "hatching an idea, and all."

"O-v-a-l. No ideas hatched in there, trust me."

"Pity," he lamented. He was referring to the egg concept, not to the lack of innovation by administrations, past, present, or future.

Arriving at the Oval Office door from the main corridor of the West Wing, Gideon knocked, confidently. After thirty seconds, he knocked again. Nothing.

"Maybe no one's home?" wondered Zebah.

"Well, let just find out, shall we?" responded Gideon. With that, he eased the door open, and poked his head in.

Seated in the room were, counterclockwise, a woman behind the John Kennedy Memorial Desk. She looked irritated. A man in uniform, with lots of colorful patches on his chest. He looked angry. A man with a writing pad. He looked confused. A woman with a silk suit, a diamond necklace so large it should have buckled her neck, and enough body work evident that her shoes should be empty. She looked *mahvelous*. Then Gideon's eyes were back to the woman and the desk. She was still irate.

"What in the blue blazes are you doing, barging into here?" inquired President Mildred Flib. "How did you get past security?" she further wondered, out loud. "If you don't leave this instant, I'll have you shot, questioned, and detained," she offered, non-sequentially.

"I'm sorry, are we interrupting anything?" asked Gideon.

"You most certainly are," Madame President replied, haughtily.

"I'm sorry, are we interrupting anything, *important*?" he clarified.

27

"You most certainly are," she responded, in kind.

"What, if I might ask, is the topic of discussion so important that we can't borrow a *smidgen* of your time?" he pressed his luck asking.

"If you must know, there's a crisis. Crises cannot be interrupted."

"Fine. But, if this is a *crisis*, and not *crises*, then, it can be interrupted, correct?" He really was curious as to this issue.

"No ... er, oh, *blast* you."

Gideon ducked, reflexively.

Nothing flew past his head. Such a relief.

"If it'll get you to leave—" the POTUS settled her nerves. "There's a crisis with a peace treaty being broken, or at least about to be broken."

"Do tell," he invited.

"Back in 1955 the tiny nation of Grand Fenwick attacked and defeated the armed forces of the United States."

"Seems implausible, but, go ahead," he requested.

"Anyway, we signed a treaty, ending the war. Now—" Madame President had to stop speaking, she was so angry. Finally, she could continue. "Now, they're threatening to renege. They want to return part of their occupied territory."

"How bad can possessing additional lands be for these united states, if I might be so bold?" he asked.

"The sole territory ceded to the tiny nation of Grand Fenwick in 1955 was the rural Jackson Township of New Jersey. Specifically, the pineland beaches."

"Pines're nice," Gideon babbled.

"I like pines, too," reinforced Zebah.

"It's where the *mobsters* are all buried. We don't want the forensic headaches back," the angry military fellow spewed. "There are more dead bodies than *clams* under those beaches. To hell with them and the Grand Fenwickians." He turned quickly to the POTUS. "They are called Fenwickians, aren't they?"

She shrugged.

"Well, this all sounds very important," allowed Gideon. "But, a quick *intermission*, if you will. My friend and I, we're aliens. Not the kind of aliens you refer to INS, or anything. No, we're *alien* aliens. Our IFO is on the South Lawn. You might have seen it?" he asked, hopefully.

"I thought it was a protest of some sort," responded President Flib."

"I thought it was one of ours," said the angry uniformed guy.

"What's an *IFO?*" asked the devil in the red dress.

"*Identified* flying object," replied Zebah, not allowing her stray-prone companion the chance.

"What's so special about an identified flying object? We all came in one. They're called *airplanes*," said the confused note taker. "You might consider getting over yourselves," he added, obnoxiously.

"Look, this is going rather sideways," complained Gideon. "We're here on Earth to get rich, quick."

Mildred Flib gestured around the room. "So are we."

"Yes, but, we don't want to expend any effort, we have no morals or scruples, and we'll take money from anyone, as long as it's given quickly and in large quantities. Strings attached are not a deterrent."

"May I get you a chair, so you might join us?" offered the POTUS.

"No, no. I'm thinking you're missing an important point. We are the representatives of a powerful group of sociopaths, anxious to destroy your planet if we do not get what we want, and we want money. *Lots* of money. We'll gladly take power, and women with bigger breasts, too, but, principally, we want cash."

"I'm not so much into the breast thing," disclaimed Zebah.

Gideon pointed to her. "I'll take her share, then."

"Look, we're all those things, too. We'll get'er done, stealing, embezzling, and skimming off profits. We're with you, baby,"

Mildred responded, getting quite excited. "And, I'm not so much into the bigger breast thing, either, but, hell yes, I'll take 'em if it affords me more stature."

"So, we want money, money, money, are unwilling to do thing one to earn it, and that's okay?" puzzled Gideon.

"Couldn't have said it better myself," replied Mildred. "In fact," she pointed to the note taker, "write than down. I'll use it."

"So, you'll give us money, money, money, no questions asked?" He tried to seal the deal.

"Hell no," laughed the president.

"But you just said—"

"I said, we're birds of a feather. What I didn't say was you could have any of ours," she gestured around the room, everyone laughing riotously, but the note taker, and the travelers.

"Son," the angry military man stated, "if you want money for nothing, you'll have to earn it the old fashioned way, all on your own."

"And, what exactly *is* the old fashioned way, er, if I might be so bold?"

"Bribes, increased taxes, and well-crafted kickbacks. Everybody knows that."

As Gideon and Zebah departed, brokenhearted, and in despair, they heard the volume of laughter only increase, the farther they went from the Oval Office.

Perhaps, Gideon reflected, Earth wasn't so very different than everywhere   else   he'd   ever   been.

CHAPTER FOUR

Dejected, our friends loitered in a shopping mall. They chose that venue because, for anyone but a fourteen-year-old girl, everyone at a shopping mall is painfully bored, depressed, or out of place. Unless, of course, you're a mall employee. They are painfully bored, depressed, *and* out of place. Anyway you measured it, the trio of travelers felt right at home. Gideon ho-hummed on a bench, occasionally sighing. Zebah stared into the window of an absurdly overpriced and under-qualitied jewelry shop. She wished she could get as much for the tasteless crap her male students had gifted her, over the years. Rigel licked ebulliently at a preposterously large lollipop and dangled his feet in the central fountain. Only one factor restrained him from complete, joyous abandon. His covert wife, Francis Jane Merryweather-Rettlebutt, couldn't be with him, on account of her having to be at work, not knowing that she was married to him, or who he was.

Assuming the others were listening, Gideon mused, "Everyone said the people of Earth were so naïve, so gullible, so ... so easy to fleece. I feel lied to."

"No, you self-deluding ball of gas," replied Zebah, "*you* are the only one who said that. We came here based on *your* vision of easy money, and no one else's."

"I bet you'd feel better if you stuck your feet in this pleasant water," bubbled Rigel.

"No, but I might if I stuck *your* head in," he responded, perking up a bit.

"You don't have to be so nasty," chided Zebah.

"Why not?" Gideon wondered. He was actually somewhat curious as to the answer.

"No one likes being made fun of or lashed out at. It's uncivil, and petty."

"Your point?"

31

"It's uncivil and petty. *That's* my point."

"But I *like* being nasty, arbitrary, and generally pissy."

"It's uncivil and it's petty."

"So am I. What, you would deny me one of my greater joys in life just because someone who is *not* me might not like or appreciate it?"

"No. What I meant to say is when's lunch? I'm starving," she seethed in resignation.

"*That's* my girl."

"I saw this restaurant down the second hall, to the left," Rigel said with a silly grin on his face. "It looked su-*perb*. The servers were all young women with fancy attire. Well, except for the fellow, dressed the same who looked awkwardly lost in time and space."

"I don't recall *any* restaurants, at all, in this wasteland of a decaying culture," observed Gideon.

"Just a few revolting fast foodless stands," added Zebah.

"I believe they call it fast *food*, not foodless," corrected Rigel.

"Have you seen what they're trying to serve? I didn't see anything *I'd* label food," scorned Zebah. When she was right, she was right.

"Be that as it may, *hater*," responded Rigel, "the restaurant I'm thinking of looks to be *sublime*. It had the cutest little face inside a circle for a logo."

"You mean Public Health stuck a skull and crossbones out front, indicating poison?" Gideon inquired, speculatively.

"No, the cutest young eunuch, with a bucket on its head. So cheery," marveled Rigel.

"Some sicko puts a bucket on a eunuch's head, adds insult to severe injury, and *you* think it's cute? I knew there was something dark inside your otherwise empty head," decried Gideon. "The poor ex-boy had a sexless, high-pitched life ahead, and you want an autographed copy of the shlock art?"

Rigel stood, involuntarily. "Do you think that's possible? I mean, not that I endorse eunuchification, or anything, but a signed copy would be *most* excellent."

"I'm sorry," Zebah huffed. "Sorry I listened to this stupid conversation, sorry that I feel the need to clarify, but, I'm sorry. Did you say you were against *unification*? The state of being brought together as one? How very odd a thing to espouse."

"No, I meant," Rigel made a scissor-like motion with two fingers, while showing something being lifted up with the other hand, "eunuch-ification."

"Oh, the times I wish I carried a hand gun," Zebah responded, in stunned disbelief.

"Show me this establishment of fine dining," proclaimed Gideon. "I am both hungry, and a man who insists on only the finest cuisine."

Rigel pointed. "Right this way."

He led the group down the main corridor, and halfway along the one to the left. Then, Rigel stopped, gestured, and glowed. "*There!*"

"Yes, I agree, not even if you *dared* me. Now, where's the restaurant you mentioned?" responded Gideon, straining to look to the right and left.

"No, *there* is the dining establishment I referred to," insisted Rigel. "Isn't it intriguing?"

"Like the dumpster out back of a morgue. Are you serious? You would *eat* that," Gideon pointed to the chief product on offer, poised at the end of a stick, "and drink that?" he swiped a hand at the tower of liquid, encased in tenuous-appearing plexiglass.

"Why not? They both appear divine."

"Meat byproducts, preservatives, antibiotics, and two percent human DNA, deep fried. Served with water the color of the ... well, it's between *orange* and *green*, on the color wheel. Haven't you heard the warning about eating the yellow snow?" challenged Gideon.

"No." Rigel looked a tad unsettled. There was a lot of frozen water in the slurry, that much was obvious.

"If the meal didn't kill you, I would, for having made *me* eat there. Hell, you want Zebah to turn back into a zombie? Hmm?"

Rigel half-pointed at the establishment. "You think those products might cause her to ... oh my."

"Oh my, my *ass*. What do you think turned the poor girl, in the first place? A virus? *Hah*. It is to laugh."

"I never gave it much thought, I guess."

"Clearly. Now, I'm so mad I have an idea. Follow me."

Gideon steamed away, determined.

"Oh, no. Now you've done it," lambasted Zebah.

"Me? What? I only suggested a lunch venue."

"No, you made him have an *idea* when *angry*. That's idengry. That's always as bad as it sounds. Last time he came up with an idengry, it cost me two toes and a month of service in a fraternity house I'd just as soon forget." Zebah was hot. "I'm holding you responsible, you got that?"

"Wh ... sure ... er, you don't think it'll end up that badly, do you?"

"If it does, *you're* wearing the chicken suit, *this* time." She heaved a tremendous breath. "Lord, how I despise the college years, fraught as they are with perverse curiosities fueled by excess alcohol."

"I wouldn't know. My parents insisted I move out as soon as I finished the minimal legal requirement. University was beyond my reach."

She looked him up and down. She started to say something, but didn't. Zebah hurried to catch up with Gideon.

Rigel reflected on loss. He'd been forced to part with his one, true love, and now, a new lunchtime experience. Which one bothered him more, he was not certain. He was only certain both were on his list.

Outside, Gideon had stopped, so the three regrouped.

"What's the plan?" asked Zebah.

"Formulating," he replied.

"There are no universities in your formulation, so far, are there?" asked a nervous Rigel.

"Universities? Man, you're loonier than ever. What do schools have to do with anything?"

"Just asking," he answered toward the ground.

"Look, we need a ride."

"To where?" asked Rigel.

Gideon returned a nasty glare. "To *not* here."

"That's going to be trouble," Zebah said instantly.

"Why? I haven't mentioned what *kind* of ride."

"Unless it's free, we can't afford it," she responded, flatly.

"Okay, we're not traveling first class. I get it. But we can afford *something*, can't we?"

"We can afford any mode of transportation as long as it's free," she insisted.

"Limiting, but not terminally so." Gideon scanned the landscape.

Fortune—not the money kind he'd have preferred, but the destiny kind—smiled upon Gideon, just then. He looked up to see he was standing next to a six-foot tall sign, reading Free IPBVFS Shuttle.

He pointed aloft. "Free transportation," he basically taunted Zebah.

"True," she spat back. "Now, if we only knew what an IPBVFS *was*, we'd know if we wanted to *go* to one."

Gideon placed a stern look on his face. He angled a thumb to the institution of over-consumption they'd recently departed. "Anything is superior to this dump."

Zebah shook her head. "*No.* You've said that, many times. Every time you do, we end up in a worse hell than the one we left behind." She crossed her arms. "Every single *freaking* time."

Turning the corner, to end their escalating spat, came a black bus, with *Complimentary IPBVFS Shuttle* plastered everywhere it could be legally affixed.

"Bingo-mania," Gideon exclaimed.

"What?" queries Rigel.

"What, what?" responded Gideon.

Zebah spoke with anger. "This sign says *Free*. The van says *Complimentary*. Those words are *similar*, but not *synonymous*."

"Of course they are," defended Gideon.

"No. Free means free. Complimentary means you're going to pay for it in some *other* manner they hope you won't notice."

"You are *so* negative. I think I liked you better when you were a zombie."

"Say that once more and you die." She was deadly serious.

Gideon gulped, in lieu of speaking a response.

"I say we take the offered rideand see what fate has in store for us."

Rigel raised a digit. "Didn't you say that the time we were nearly killed by the rabid dogs in Omaha?"

"And when we were nearly killed by a one-winged bat, or those bowls of predatory fruit, and, of course, whenever we visit your mother," pressed Zebah.

"No way. The mom-thing was more personal and directed at *me*, not *us*. It's unfair to include it on that other, alleged list of near-misses."

"You're right. The fact that your mother launched a tactical nuclear weapon at *you*, when we were traveling *with* you, does suggest Rigel and I were not the *intended*, only the *unintended*, targets."

"See. So, in summary, the alleged list of near-death experiences is as short as it is alleged."

"You know, it's at times like this *I* wish I were a zombie again," she hissed. "That way, when I chewed your still-beating heart out of your chest, no one would move to convict me."

Gideon wagged a finger at the minibus. "Uh, as much as I'd love to continue this stroll down memory lane, the bus appears to be ready to depart. Shouldn't we board?"

"Maybe you can, while we stand here and wave goodbye?" volunteered Zebah.

Gideon shook his head. "No. You'd miss me, too much, too soon."

Zebah looked to Rigel. "You willing to take that risk?"

"What could go wrong that we haven't already cataloged?"

"You guys are a ball of laughs. Really. Cripplingly so, in fact. But I have a feeling this minibus is our portal to *unbelievable* success," responded Gideon.

"Then you should board it," Zebah challenged, crossing her arms and angling her head.

"Ah, here's the thing of it. I'd feel bad, leaving you two behind."

Zebah glanced incredulously at Rigel, who returned, in kind, the look and the sentiment.

"Write if you find work," stated Zebah flatly.

"The reasons I'd feel just terrible leaving you behind are these." He reached into his coat pocket and produced a couple boxes of golf balls and one of tees.

Zebah chuckled, sarcastically. "That crap. We're not going with you because you have that."

"Perhaps I need to expand upon my reasoning here. Do you see those young men trotting toward us?"

They turned, then turned back.

"So?" shot Zebah.

"I can't be certain from this distance, but I *believe* they represent the mall's security service."

"You stole that crap?" wheezed Zebah. "You don't even *play* golf."

"I was hoping to learn, someday. Possibly."

"Ooooh. You *so* infuriate me," she volcanoed.

"Might I talk you into being *so infuriated,* on the Complimentary IPBVFS Shuttle?"

"Oooooh, you make me so mad, too," grumbled Rigel.

They boarded the bus, Gideon encouraging them, energetically.

Gideon placed a hand on the drivers shoulder. "Do you see those three men, there, the one's rushing this minibus?"

"Ya," he replied defiantly.

"They are an STD gang. They roam the streets, hoping to inflict new STDs on everyone they can capture. If I were you, and if I did not want any new diseases, I'd close the door and drive away as quickly as possible."

The driver did just that. Mind you, he was a bitter, disbelieving misanthrope, in general. Seriously, he was a heel's heel, a wretched man in the body of a disgruntled man, masquerading as someone able to function in a public venue. But he was also one who did not wish to explain to his wife, for the fifth time, how he *accidentally* got a new STD. Times one through four were bad enough, thank you very much.

The IPBVFS turned out to be very close. The minibus made the turn into its sweeping driveway, lined with trees and seasonal flowers. Gideon beheld such a sight, one not only for his sore eyes, but for his predatory swindling instincts. For, in tasteful lettering along an arched-metal entry portal, was the full name of the business so nice as to provide a complimentary shuttle service. The Institute of Psychic Bankers and Visionary Financial Seers welcomed any, and all, to its doors.

Gideon wiped the small tear away that had formed in the corner of his left eye. Then he turned to his friends. He was so emotionally

38

revved-up, he could hardly speak. But, "hardly" wasn't enough to prevent him from gushing, "I'm home."

The ever vigilant Zebah had also already seen the sign and placed two and two together. She knew her man was going to lose all the pittance of the self-control he possessed. Gideon would be, absolutely and unequivocally, smitten and overwhelmed by the prospect of attending this august institution. She'd have more luck stopping a locomotive by throwing her body in front of it, as it powered down the tracks, than impeding Gideon from going, instantly, all in.

For the record, Rigel was hangry, and didn't even notice they'd turned off the main road. He wanted, in no particular order, his hot dog on a wooden pole, his non-wife, his immense lollipop back, and a pony. The pony thing, that was some childhood fixation, not part of the current reality he was doing such a proud job of ignoring as an adult.

The bus stopped before an imposing set of stairs that led up to the highly decorated doors that marked the entryway into TIPBVFS. The driver slammed open the door, and, without even a glance backward, yelled, "Everybody off. We're here."

"What's your next stop, driver?" asked a nervous Zebah.

That got the man's head to halfway rotate. "It's a mystery to you and yours, since you're getting off here, *now*. This ain't no free *ride*, sister. It's complimentary."

She turned to beg, threaten, and generally cajole Gideon into remaining on the bus. Too late. He was already gone. Zebah bolted out the door and caught him just as he was about to ascend the steps to his future, to his destiny.

"Gideon, I know what you're thinking, but no. The answer is *no*. Hell, the question is *no*. We're not throwing what little money remains to us in this universe at a bunch of con men." She jumped in front of him, straddling his waist with her legs, as Gideon hadn't even slowed. She shouted in his face. "Honey, we're the cons. We don't *fall* for them."

But her words were as unheard as they were unheeded. Gideon, wearing Zebah in front, opened the door and entered the not-so-hallowed halls of TIPBVFS. Gideon trembled, he was so stricken. In awe, he approached the desk, at the rear of the over-decorated, garish vestibule. It was done in a sort of Louis-XIV-arm-wrestling-with-Liberace style. Migraine sufferers, and anyone with a modicum of taste, be warned.

The woman behind the counter was smiling at Gideon/Zebah, as they approached. They had her fullest attention. She was a real pro.

"Good afternoon," she greeted with a motherly, yet BFF intonation. This one was a *consummate* pro. "We knew you were coming," she gestured seamlessly to indicate a pitcher of once-ice water, a small stack of styrofoam cups by its side, "so we prepared a refreshment just for you two."

"Nice pitch, sweet cheeks," snarled Zebah, as she bypassed Gideon. "But there's three of us. One's too dimwitted to enter of his own accord."

"And, knowing such was the case, in advance, is why we prepared no refreshment for *him*."

Gideon's eyes met Zebah's. They were both most impressed. The girl was top-flight.

"I don't know about you," Gideon remarked to Zebah as he headed to the cheap-imitation-of-a-rococo console table, "but I'm starving." He poured himself a glass of room-temperature water and devoured it with gusto. "Ah, did that hit the spot, or what?"

"We aim to please, sir. My name is Uwanitt Ugottit, but *you* may call me, simply, Ms. *Ugottit*."

"You got it, doll," Gideon said, with a snap of the fingers, and a point at her.

Zebah balled up her fists, while rolling her eyes. This, make no mistake about it, was war.

"Are you here to invest with the Psychic Bank, or are you hoping to enroll in our visionary financial advisor's instructional program?"

"Why you asking, bitch?" snapped Zebah. "Thought you knew it all."

"First off, I knew you'd say that. Second, I know the answer, but, as the psychically gifted can be quite intimidating, we have learned to keep that horse in the barn, more often than not."

The travelers exchanged another glance of awed reverence for the master of her art form, Ms. Ugottit.

"Actually, neither. I'm here looking to add my name to TIPBVFS' list of distinguished faculty."

Betty Anne Vigros, for that was the real name of the woman purporting to be Ms. Ugottit, immediately switched gears. She went from butter'em-up-and-keep-them-from-leaving, to take-a-number-and-STFU in one brief, dismissive moment. "Do you have an appointment?" she asked in a raspy Brooklyn accent.

"Don't you *know* all and *see* all?" taunted Zebah.

Betty Anne raised her pen to shoulder height and made a show of dropping it to the desktop. "If I needed someone to give me crap, I'd have not dumped all my exes. Trust me, they were all a hell of a lot cuter than you, toots. If someone's going to ruin my mood, they might as well be easy on the eyes."

Zebah could not argue that excellent point, so she let it drop.

"In point of fact," Gideon spoke up, eagerly, "I do not exactly have an *appointment*. But," he raised a finger, "that is only because, up until this very moment, I was unaware of TIPBVFS' existence."

Betty Anne stared at Gideon, in disbelief. "When you were scanning the want ads this morning, did you mistake the call for 'No skills required, but must be good with people' to somehow be from us at TIPBVFS?"

"You are a sharp tack, Ms. Ugottit," he genuinely praised. "I can see we will get along swimmingly as near-coworkers. I, as professor, and you as my quick-witted assistant. *Nice*."

"Don't get ahead of yourself and strain a neuron, pal," she responded. "I can buzz the boss and ask him if he has time that he wishes to flush completely down the toilet by talking with you."

"She's good. I need people like that protecting me," he marveled to Zebah.

As the only one even possibly regarded to be "his people," she was not positively inclined, upon hearing that praise.

Betty Anne thumbed the intercom. "Hello, Dr. Miraculous," she punched the desktop with her free hand, "I mean, *Slube*, there's a grifter what wants a piece of your hard earned action out here. Do you wants that I have Eloise release the dogs on him and his demented looking groupies?"

Rigel, who'd finally entered, leaned into Zebah. "Gideon has groupies? Why don't *I* know anything about this? I spend almost every waking hour with the man."

She looked at him as if he were a complete idiot.

"Ah, I got a sec," Slube said, rather vacantly. "Show him in, but just the one. And buzz me in three minutes to tell me my wife's on fire. I don't want to waste too much of my designated farting-time on this loser."

"You know he's right in front of me and can hear you plain as I can?"

"I *assumed* no less," Slube answered with surprise in his voice.

"The boss'll see you, but do us all a favor and keep it short."

"Not to worry. If I can't convince him I'm a necessary part of TIPBVFS' future in less than three minutes, I'm losing my touch."

"Whatever." She pointed with her pen. "Second door on the left. Knock once, then in you go."

"Second, left, once. Got it."

42

"Thanks for sharing," she responded with no interest.

Gideon stepped into Slube's office, as instructed. The room was seven, maybe eight times more hideous than the entry vestibule. The lousy copies of distinguished furniture were the same pathetic quality, but, in here, they were crammed together like the deckchairs on the Titanic.

A short, squat man sat behind a deck that must have been designed to serve a dual function as a workspace and a defensible barrier. Gideon's entry didn't attract any attention from Slube, in spite of the fact that he was basically just staring off into space.

Finally, the boss yawned, scratched his crotch, and looked toward Gideon. "Grab a seat."

"Why, thank you, Slube. You don't mind if I call you Slube, do you, Slube?"

"Couldn't care less. So what makes you think I might possibly need you here to dilute my portion of the take?"

"An excellent question. You see, it's like this—"

"Wait, wait. I forget to ask. What's your name? I'm Slube Vacantly. It's spelled like there's no one home, but it's pronounced like I said it, Va-*can't*-ly."

Gideon sucked in his lower lip. Oh my, he reflected. "Why not just change the spelling to match the pronunciation that is your destination?"

"I'm presupposing you haven't met my dad, SluborVacantly?"

"I imagine I'd recall that name."

"If I were to change my name, even slightly from the family standard, dad'd be displeased."

"Is that a terribly bad thing?"

"Do you recall that town out west that disappeared without a trace, a few years back?"

"Sorry, can't say that I do."

"I want you to take one wild guess at who got a parking ticket there only hours before the Earth swallowed the place up."

"Ah. Well, fortunately for us all, your last name is a winner. I may change to it, myself."

"Sure, pal. How about the name? You're two minutes into three, already."

Gideon rose and extended his hand. "I'm Gideon Prime. Pleased to meet you, Slube."

Staring at the hand, held in mid air, Slube said, "So, why is it I need you?"

"Well, I'm not one to toot my own horn. Not often, that is. But, it's fair to say I've ... er, dabbled in the field you're currently plowing. I—"

"Hang on," Slube said, massaging his forehead. "Gideon Prime?"

"That's me."

"*The* Gideon Prime, Prime?"

"No. I'm just Gideon Prime, once. You must be thinking of someone else."

He snapped his fingers. "*The* Gideon Prime who made a fortune selling the franchise rights for self-service mortuaries? *The* Gideon Prime who basically invented drive thru hemorrhoid surgery? *The* Gideon Prime who sold freezers to half the population of Tothe, aka The *Ice* Planet?"

"I had a few good weeks there, back to back, I will admit."

"A few good weeks," Slube scoffed incredulously. "I believe it's called global *warming* on a massive scale, my friend."

Gideon almost blushed. "Truth be told, what I did to those polar ice caps was *pretty* clever, if I do say so, myself."

"*Sir*," Slube stood and reached a hand across the desk, "it would be my honor and my privilege to learn at the side of a master such as yourself. Consider us equal partners as of immediately."

"Wow. Just, wow," Gideon responded. "You knew about all that?"

"Say, now that I'm opening my mental Gideon Prime File, weren't you working on a friendly-welcoming-affordable-legal-services scam?"

Gideon shook his head. He was pained to recall that venture, that albatross that never could take wing. "You know, Slube, if there's absolutely no credibility in the hustle, there's no buy-in. From the get-go, not a single person believed such a creature existed."

"Did seem a *bit* farfetched, I must admit."

"But ... how could you know of my ... my *accomplishments*? We're still on Earth, right?"

"Of course we are. But, please know, sir, when true brilliance, shear genius is at play, word spreads. Reputations precede great men, always."

"Well, color me flattered."

"I will," replied Slube.

"Imagine that."

"Imagine that," echoed Slube.

Down to business like a lion holding a zebra's windpipe between its jaws, Gideon pressed. "So, what's your scam, here, Slube?"

He sat back and gloated. "Oh, your *typical* investment scam, I suppose. I'd like to think there's some unexpected money nonsense," he shuffled his fingers, "mixed with *just* enough fortune-telling mumbo-jumbo to keep it fresh."

"Sounds *intriguing*."

"Thank you. Coming from you, that's high praise."

Gideon looked to the side and placed a few knuckles against his lips.

"We've—*we* being me, Eloise, whom you haven't met, and Betty Anne, whom you have met—been at this only a short while. We've sown a lot of seeds, but not harvested much hard cash, as of yet."

Gideon looked all around the room. "You gotta be kidding me. This place looks legit."

"Really. Awe, shucks, now I'm going to blush. It's a work in progress."

"Seriously," encouraged Gideon. "Sure, I'm looking at a place stuffed to the rafters with tasteless *crap*. But, pal-o-matic, this much used horseshit would cost appreciable green money. Don't be shy and self-effacing. It's beneath you."

"We did have a leg up. Normally I wouldn't admit it, but we were running the rather amateurish lonely heart scam on the old goat who owned this place," Slube swept a hand around, generally. "But, before Betty Anne had her bra half off, the loser died of a stroke, or something."

"Really. The doctors couldn't tell?" wondered Gideon, in spite of his callous disregard for anyone who wasn't him.

"No, mostly because we buried him out back under the croquet court. No next of kin nagging at the authorities, either."

"Sweet, squared."

"Tell me about it. So, until someone the hell notices that the late and apparently completely unlamented Reginald Prattfield-Maugham is missing, we can run our action off his estate."

"There is a God," declared Gideon. "I don't care what anyone says."

"I got you an *amen*, Brother Gideon."

"So, how many takers for the psychic banking crap?"

"Oh, a dozen, mostly mental weak-links with more money than common sense."

"Excellent combination. Good work."

"Thanks. But, I think we need some major capital to prime—no pun intended—this project."

"Hmm," Gideon offered blandly. "Sufficient funding can be a challenge. I've had many an otherwise brilliant scheme torpedoed by insufficient funding."

The conversation lagged at that point. Gideon lost in personal reflections and an odd preoccupation of picturing Betty Anne half-out of her brassiere. Not that the woman was fetching, well-endowed, or in any way charming, but that image lingered, nonetheless.

Slube was quietly analyzing Gideon. You know how an eagle studies a fish just under the surface of the water, determining what, if any, angle would best serve to remove said fish from said body of water? Yeah, in that way the host inspected the guest.

"You ever attempt a job like this one, oh wise and resourceful Gideon?"

"Well," he waved the back of a hand in the air, "when I was young, I suppose. I've never been very interested in long hustles. Never saw the percentages, truth be told. And my middling case of AHDH doesn't help, I'm told." He harrumphed quietly. *"Doctors."*

"You know, I cut my teeth, so to speak, under the tutelage of none other than Nihal 110?"

"No," replied Gideon, astounded and impressed. *"The* Nihal 110, Natwarlal, the man who repeatedly sold the Taj Mahal, the Red Fort, the Rashtrapati Bhavan, and the Parliament House of India?"

Slube leaned back and beamed. "The one and the same."

"So you *know* long term cons."

"Like they were my own babies." The eagle committed to a flight plan. "You know, I'm pretty much tapped out, here." He gestured to the general space surrounding him. "I mean, sure, we have a little income, but no payday's in sight, if you know what I mean?"

"Oh, I feel your pain, brother."

"If somehow I could put my hands ... what am I saying? Our hands on a modest sum, I really think the psychic banking thing'd take off like a Saturn 5 rocket."

"*Actual* money," scorned Gideon. "It's such a bitch."

"Say, you wouldn't happen to own a spaceship, would you?"

Ah, Gideon thought, he was looking in a mirror, here. This man didn't think he could romance his ship away, did he? Ha. Coals to Newcastle were the words that came to Gideon's mind.

"I *am* an alien visitor to Earth."

"Is it a big ship, a nice ship?"

"Oh, I don't know. It gets me from here to there. But, it's not luxurious or *particularly* big."

"Well, you see, I have this friend."

Gideon shuddered. "Don't we all?"

"The point is, my friend has some boxes. He wishes to get those boxes from Point A, to Point B."

"Bleh," was Gideon's response.

"Unfortunately, due to the prejudices and turbulence of the times we live in, the government of Point B regards the contents of the boxes sitting in a warehouse in Point A as less than desirable."

"You mean illegal?"

"Another term for it, thank you."

"We're talking smuggling, here, right?"

"*Smuggling.* It has such a legal-sounding undertone. I call it shipping and receiving. The major players of industry do it on a daily basis."

"Bottom line me, here, Slube. While we're still young."

"If you could used your spaceship to transfer a small number of my friend's boxes—wooden boxes, mind you—to a predetermined location, my friend would then have the free cash to lend us some, so we can start a proper Ponzi scam, here."

"Wooden boxes?" he made an estimation of their size, in the air between them.

Slube bobbed his head. "Some are similar to what you describe."

"But some aren't?"

"You have such a fluid mind. No, some have ... alternative shapes."

"Such as?"

"Some of the wooden boxes are neither wood, nor boxes. They're more like boxes with arms and legs, boxes that speak only a foreign language, most of the time."

"Human trafficking? That's what we're actually talking about, right?"

"*Boxes*, friend Gideon. Remember. Only. Wooden. Boxes."

"Just boxes. Got you."

"Of course, a few of the wooden boxes look all the world like metal cylinders. *Warm* metal cylinders."

"How is it that those *metal* wooden boxes find themselves warm?"

"They might, by some definitions, contain concentrated nuclear waste. Allegedly. Focus on that rationalization, and you'll be fine."

"*Allegedly* hazardous materials—in wooden boxes," echoed Gideon.

"So, if, say, you were to pick up this handful of wooden boxes, and, with the use of your advanced-alien-technology spacecraft, reposition these wooden crates, we would have more than enough start-up capital to make TIPBVFS a real powerhouse. Hell, we could maybe even start printing up those degrees I designed."

"To dream well is to dream big."

Slube pointed right at Gideon. "I knew I liked you, right outta the gate."

"So, where do I locate, and relocate to, this handful of wooden boxes?"

"The items in question are currently in a warehouse in a blessedly chaotic, yet repressively governed country somewhat *south* of this great nation."

"Perfect. And the destination?"

"Have you ever heard of Paramus?"

"The one where Mr. Rizzo lives and plies his dubious trade?"

Slube nearly exploded with glee. "This is getting easier, and easier. You two are friends."

"Hmm. *Friend* is not the optimal word, but it is in the same galactic lexicon, if one pushes at the boundaries of meaning."

"Close enough for my peace of mind, I can tell you with certainty." Slube was really upbeat. It pleased Gideon that he was making such a good early impression with his new partner.

Only then did Gideon insist Zebah and Rigel meet their new associate. Hindsight, damnable, accursed hindsight, is always so much more crippling, than foresight. If Gideon had brought his friends in *earlier* in the budding business deal, matters might have ended ... oh, let's just say it—better. Acceptably. Non-life-threateningly. But if life were easy, anyone could do it well.

Three days later, Gideon and his crew had moved the seven hundred individual pieces, or persons, of wooden boxes from a third world spit-hole to Mr. Rizzo's two main warehouses, just outside of Paramus. Some initial delay occurred, inevitably, based on Mr. Rizzo's forces firing upon Gideon, when first they saw him. Those were standing orders in Paramus. After some tense negotiations, and no small amount of first aid, Gideon was allowed to offload his shipment. Then, after more shooting, and more first aid, the crew narrowly escaped with their lives. That Mr. Rizzo held quite the grudge was proven in that encounter.

To Gideon's surprise, when he passed through the stately entrance of TIPBVFS, four days hence, he was greeted not with a vision of Betty Anne, bra fully in place. No, he spied a thin male

50

figure in a dark suit clearly purchased with economy, not fashion, in mind.

"Hi, pally," chortled Gideon. "You the new guy?"

The man labored to raise his large head. As mirthlessly as a corpse, he replied, "No."

"I'm Gideon. Where's ... ah, where's Slube?"

"To whom are you referring?" replied the emaciated remnants of a human, seated there, behind the desk.

"Ah," he tapped the side of his nose. "You're right. Where's Dr. Miraculous?"

"To whom are you referring?"

"The administrator of this little gold mine, pally cake. Where's the boss?"

"Are you possibly referring to the late Mr. Reginald Prattfield-Maugham, recently exhumed from the croquet pitch?"

"Court, silly. It's a court, not a pitch."

"I stand corrected."

"So, who the hell are you?" Gideon demanded.

"Ah, allow me to introduce myself. I am Hardly Athing. I'm an accountant employed by the law firm of Stahl, Delay, and Bill-Allot. We are executors for the estate of the aforementioned decedent."

"Where's ... where *is* Slube Vacantly?" Gideon asked, uncertainly.

"Is that a jest?"

"Is what a jest?"

"That surname."

"I'm not sure you are in a position to pose such a question, my man."

"Point. I may bear some pleasant news, however," said Hardly, straining to smile, yet failing at it completely.

"Unlikely, but shoot."

Zebah and Rigel, who hadn't sprinted from the car, entered the vestibule.

"What's up?" asked Zebah. "Who's this stiff?"

"Hardly Athing," Gideon replied, absently.

"No kidding. Hey, small thin puke," she pressed, "you got a name?"

"No, babe," explained Gideon, "his name's *Hardly*, but you can ignore his existence."

Hardly angled his head, ever so slightly. "Most people do."

"Where's Slube?"

"We don't know. Not here, apparently," Gideon replied sheepishly.

"Didn't I mention—"

"But, someone else is, right, Hardly?"

"Yes. I was told it was your confessor."

"My what? Don't recall ever having one of those."

Hardly shrugged. He didn't know, either way.

"Well, bring whoever it is out," snarled Zebah.

"I was instructed to have you go to him. He's in that closet over there. Step in, close the door, and turn on the light."

"Are you sure, dude?" pressed Gideon. "Kind of strange venue and set of instructions."

"That was what I was told."

"By whom?" asked Rigel.

"The man who called about an hour ago."

"Who was the man who called an hour ago?" continued Rigel.

"*About* an hour ago," corrected Hardly.

"Name. What was the man's name?"

"He didn't say. He simply gave me those instructions, chuckled as if he were not mentally all there, and then he hung up on me." Hardly looked away. "Most people do."

"Okay, let's get this over with," sighed Gideon.

The three crowded into the closet, closed the door, and hit the light switch.

Swobo Grabski flashed to life. He held *two* machetes overhead, poised to strike. Both were covered in crusted blood. He said something along the lines of, "Dieeeeeee—

Then he charged.

Do you remember those scenes in *The Three Stooges* where they all tried to exit a door at once and got stuck? Yeah, form that mental image. Then add Swobo beginning the downward arch of his deadly weapons. Now color in the three pushing so hard the door frame snaps free. End your mental image with a woman, and two men, wearing a door frame, running across a lawn. A very angry, primal man with two raised machetes, is giving chase. Everyone in the image is screaming, but, clearly, for different reasons.

Fade   to   black.

CHAPTER FIVE

"Would you *please*, for the love of all that's holy, stop humming that tune?" Gideon was beside himself with irritation.

"Really," replied a demure Zebah. "Don't tell me I doing it *again*?"

"You know *perfectly* well you were."

And she did. In the hours that followed their narrow escape from the insane Swobo, Zebah had composed a little song, perhaps a jingle, immortalizing the fact that Gideon Prime had been conned, but good. It was simple in its composition. It went:

"Gideon got swin-dled,
Gideon got swin-dled,"
(then the performer does an air hip bump)
"Oh, yeah, he got conned real good."

The melody, if it can be said to rise to that standard, was equally ... simple. It was, in fact childish and grating. But Zebah so loved her opus. She loved it because it got so far under Gideon's skin, so quickly, she was enraptured. She would sing quietly to herself, until he scolded her, demanding she stop that instant. Then, she'd switch over to the humming, or whistling, of the tune. Wash. Rinse. Repeat. Rigel even found he was sucked into the plot, though unconsciously. Most things Rigel did were unconscious. When the two of them joined in concert, Gideon went ballistic. That gave Zebah such great joy, she privately compared it to the feeling she often got after working with one of her well-endowed clients.

"Look, I'm not out any actual cash. I performed a bit of labor, *gratis*. That's all," he huffed, time and again. "It's actually a valuable lesson. Stay alert, Gideon. There are bad people out there."

"Yes, and at least one of them is *proven* to be more clever than you," Zebah would try to say, while gasping a laugh.

"No money lost equals no actual sting, honey babe. You know that."

"Let's see, you risk life and limb and Slube gets paid. How's that not a money-loss scenario on your part?"

"Because I came out with as much cash as I had to begin with."

"Which is nothing, you're broke, and you were conned."

"When will you be *dropping* this minor setback?"

"I don't know. When will you be *dying*?" She snickered shamelessly.

He glared at her, long and hard. "We need to begin setting in place the means for us to secure some funds."

"Oh, why? Is Slube coming by to purloin that, too, soon?"

"No," he growled through gritted teeth. "Because we're out of milk and dangerously low on tea, itself."

"And the "F" word. Don't forget the "F" word."

"I'm certain you'll be addressing it to me often."

"I meant *food*, as in, we have no food, either."

"I am aware of our ship's stores issues."

"And, don't forget that ..."

"Gideon got swin-dled,
Gideon got swin-dled,"
(then the performer does an air hip bump)
"Oh, yeah, he got conned real good."

"Unless you enjoy being strangled in your sleep, I suggest you never sing that insult again."

"What song are you referring to? Rigel, do you know what melodic interlude Gideon is referencing?"

"I believe so. It's ..."

"Gideon got swin-dled,

Gideon got swin-dled,"
(then Rigel did an air hip bump)
"Oh, yeah, he got conned real good."

"Is that the one, Giddy?" she asked, with tenderness and empathy.

"Plans. We need plans."

"You're probably right," she admitted. "Do you have any ideas?"

"None, per se."

"What, Gideon, does that mean, precisely?" asked a timid Rigel.

"It means he's got no clue," defined Zebah. "Unless you or I come up with something, we'll starve to death, homeless, while we're dressed in hand-me-down rags."

"Don't be so dramatic," snapped Gideon. "I always come up with something."

"Yeah ... That's usually when the trouble begins, too," observed a fatigued Zebah.

"I have a thought," announced Rigel.

"Take two aspirin, then two more, then the rest of the bottle. The sensation will pass quickly enough," grumbled Gideon.

"What, Mr. None, Per Se? If you got nothing, at least we could hear the man out."

"Thank you," responded Rigel, surprise evident in his tone.

"Then we ridicule him and mock him to within an inch of his life," she added.

"And why are we stopping that inch shy of freedom?" posed Gideon.

"You two do know I have feelings, right?" asked a wounded Rigel.

"Your point being?" inquired Gideon.

"Stop, stop," blurted Zebah. "Rigel, what is your idea to keep us from life-foreclosure?"

"Why don't we get actual jobs, real jobs. We could ... what do they call it? Ah, yes. We could *work* for a living."

Zebah and Gideon exchanged incredulous glances.

"I suppose this is where you begin inching me toward death," Rigel mused, mostly to himself.

Gideon scanned the room for a weapon, or a projectile. There it was. A hammer, small, but well balanced.

"You know what?" asked Zebah, loudly.

Gideon ignored her. He was ready to rumble.

"I say *again*, you know what?"

"Huh, er, what?" stammered Gideon.

"I've done a lot of things in my life, most of which I'm not particularly proud of. But you know what I've never, ever done?"

Gideon set down his hammer. "This'll be good," he told himself, lustfully. "And, we can do it later, to dispel your current regrets." The man was a pig, plain and simple.

She scowled at him. "I've never done an honest day's work."

"And—" invited Gideon, as he wiped saliva from his cheeks.

"And nothing. That's it. I've never worked an honest job, *once*."

"Nor have I, but you don't see me trumpeting that accomplishment in a public square."

"No. What I mean is, what the heck? Let's give regular work, the old nine-to-five, a chance. What's the worst that could happen?"

"The worst that could happen. Child, bite your tongue, or I'll bite it for you. The worst that could ... oh, I can't even think the words. The worst that could happen is we'd like being gainfully employed and we'd continue upon that career path until a sensible, early retirement." He trembled violently. Goosebumps formed atop the goosebumps that'd already erupted.

"Wait, your vision of the *worst* possible outcome is that you'd settle down and lead a productive life?"

He slammed his palms to his ears. "Stop *saying* those words. I'm going insane."

"Talk about your over-reacting job," she scoffed.

"Job, job, job. Stop *cursing* in my presence."

A bucket of lukewarm water splashed into Gideon's face. He saw Zebah standing there, an enormous grin on her face, and a wash bucket in her hands.

"Why did you splash me with wash-water?"

"I didn't splash you with wash-water."

He pointed. "Yes you did. You're holding a wash bucket."

"It was the nearest thing, so I grabbed it. I had to get enough toilet water to drench you."

"I know where we might apply for entry-level positions," Rigel spoke up, hoping to stem the mayhem.

"Oh, yeah," taunted Gideon. "I think we'd better refer that issue to *Zebah*. She's a pro when it comes to entry-level positions." He laughed sarcastically at his witticism. Doubled over, cackling like a maniac, he felt a second wave, though lesser in volume, splash against his face, and something seemed to have stuck to the tip of his nose.

"Oh no. More toilet water," he mocked. "Boo, hoo, hoo."

"Nah," she responded, letting the remark hang in the air a moment. "That one's special delivery from just little old *me*."

"I thought you said we were going to get jobs in some food-producing place, not some religious temple," complained Gideon.

"We are. This *is* a restaurant."

"Really, with those shiny arches we passed under? That's a temple, in my book."

"Maybe it's a temple to fine dining?" speculated Zebah.

"Is your nose functioning, my dear?" asked Gideon.

"Yes. Why?"

"Then how could you employ the words *fine* or *dining*. Here it's food-slopping of the great unwashed."

"Someone's in an unusually pissy mood, today," she observed.

"Shush, both of you. We must be on our best behavior if we're to secure employment here." Rigel studied the expansive room. He walked up to the counter. "Excuse me ... er, Rachel B.," he said, reading her name tag, "how might we go about securing employment in this restaurant?"

She eyed him, dubiously. "Can you read?" she challenged.

"I'd like to think so."

"Can you enter a door while reading?" she pressed.

"I ... I, uh, don't know. I've never tried that trick, specifically."

"Then we've arrived at your lucky day." She pointed. "Walk out those doors. Then, walk back in those doors, while reading all the signs you see from that vantage point. Do you think you can do that for me?"

Rigel went down a mental checklist. Out door, in door, read door. Got it. "Got it."

"I'm marking this day on my calendar," she snarked back.

"Thank you," Rigel beamed. He wasn't sure why she needed to write today into today's date on her calendar, but she sure seemed nice about letting him know she was.

After exiting, Rigel spun, cheerily, and reentered the establishment. He read as he did so. HOURS OF SERVICE. Yes, interesting reading. NO PETS. Hmm. Fascinating. The restaurant didn't sell pets. Good to know. NO SHIRT, NO SHOES, NO SERVICE. My, that was going to take a while to decipher. Was it free-form poetry? A mantra? Could it be a request? No, shirt, as in, shirt, do not do that? Sentient clothing? Was that what the sign suggested? Maybe they did not serve shirts -- *NO, shirt, stop eating that food item?* Most peculiar.

Ah, there was the one his new friend must have been referring to. All Job Applicants Please Do So Online. Excellent. Rigel was now informed. He stepped up to the counter. "Rachel B., I'm ready to apply for a job. Where is the line into which I get?" He smiled, proud that he'd understood the facts of the process so quickly.

"You again?"

"Me what again?"

"You here again?"

"Yes. You are quite perceptive. Now, the *on* line."

"No, simple man, you have to apply online, just like I did, just like everybody does."

"I can hardly wait. Which line is it?"

"Are you mental?"

Mental? Was he ... psychic? "No, Rachel B. But, wouldn't it be wonderful if I was? What if we all were?" He sighed, thinking of such a wonderful world.

"Yup, you're mental."

Rigel blushed. "I'm so glad you think I am." He waved a hand between them. "It really strengthens our bond."

"We do not have a bond. You so much as touch me, and you'll find out why God gave a woman knees."

Touch her, and God would speak to him about ... the reasons for female anatomy? Earth was more peculiar than he'd suspected. But direct contact with a deity, that would be nice. Rigel reached across and touched Rachel B.'s shoulder. Then he readied himself for the divine.

Eyes closed, arms raised toward Heaven, Rigel stool there, with an unsuppressable grin on his face. He was interrupted, however, not by the spoken word of God, but by the impact of the milkshake machine against his chest. Rachel B. had been aiming for Rigel's head, but the machine was quite heavy. She performed, actually, impressively.

"What the hell's going on out here," shouted a boy of twelve, Rigel estimated. He wore part of the uniform the other employees wore, but his was filthy, and his fly was unzipped.

"Sorry, Mr. Pimples ... I mean Mr. Pomple. This man touched me so I threw that machine at him."

"Not the knee, this time?" Gerald F. Pomple, the assistant shift manager, was thinking back how he'd received a knee for his "accidental" groping of Rachel. Come on, he whined in his head. It was an *accident.* Her left breast was *directly* between him and the soda dispenser, more or less, during the lunch rush. Gerald, it should be noted, spoke in a perpetual, insufferable whine, even in his head. Upon first hearing him, Gideon was certain Gerald was from the planet Grim. There, everyone spoke in varied intonations of a whine, with an occasional snivel, and a rare, but unmistakable, complete emotional collapse bracketed in four words or less. But, Gideon realized Gerald couldn't be Grimmarian. For one thing, Gerald had no obvious tentacles, and clearly had but one head. Also, the collective population of Grim was so ... let's just say it, *grim*, that they decided breeding wasn't worth listening to their mates whining the entire time. (Faster. Slower. You're not nearly the male my last mate was. You call *those* appendages? Et cetera.) Hence, over a thousand years ago, the species became, to the lamentation of no one, extinct.

"No, sir." She pointed to the counter.

"Look, I'm sure this paying customer didn't mean to touch you."

"Oh, no," exuded Rigel. "I wanted to hear God speak to me, as she promised."

Gerald leaned in close to Rigel. "Trust me on this, buddy. The guys who work here that are in a position to know say she ain't capable of that."

"But she said—"

"Is there a problem here?" asked Gideon. He'd been happy to watch Rigel bungle, up to that point.

"No problem, pops," responded Gerald. "Simple misunderstanding. Now, why don't you all place your orders. I'll see to it that they're prepared real special for you."

"The boy's a peach," Rigel said glowingly, as he pointed to the assistant manager.

"We are not here to dine. We are here to apply for jobs on line. Do you know where that line is?" Rigel asked pleasantly.

"I'm confused," replied Gerald.

Rigel held out a hand. "Nice to meet you, Confused."

"No, I'm not named confused, I am in the state of confusion." He threw his arms up. "And before you say no, we're not, this is Kansas—don't."

"I'm learning so much I feel I should be paying you," Rigel responded, with pep.

"Whatever. Look, guys, normally you have to apply online. That way, I can say I lost your application, not that I *actually* only want to hire babes, not dudes. However, I'm critically short at this moment. Necessity is the mother of need, as they say."

"I want to go on record as feeling you are short, yes. But critically so? Never. You're cute, in a gnomish kind of way," complimented Rigel. Or so he thought.

"I have half a mind to pick up that milkshake machine and use it myself," Gerald declared, angrily.

"Well, when you're as *short* as you are," Gideon speculated, "half a brain is *probably* all you really require."

Gerald's anger flared, but then, like a campfire in a deluge, it sputtered out. He was instantly bored. Boredom was his only friend. "Look, you guys want the jobs, yes or no?"

"So, you're offering us jobs, on the condition our attitude is yes or no? I'm not certain what that means," stated Rigel.

"If you're that dumb, you'll work out fine, here. Grab some uniforms from the pile in the back room. Try and at least get the *gender* right, okay?"

"We will get our genders right, sir," declared Rigel. "When does our training begin?"

"Training's over. Now's the part where you get your asses to work," spat Gerald.

"What work do you want our asses to do, boss?" Rigel was concerned.

Zebah stepped forward and rested a hand on Rigel's chest. "Not to worry, little Gerald. I'll in-service him."

"I like that. A girl with initiative. And, for an old lady, you're not too ugly." He rubbed his chin. "Say, would you like to help me with a problem I'm having, in my office?"

Zebah rolled her eyes. "Sure thing. The minute you hit puberty, we'll get to work on that little problem of yours."

"Come with me, you three idiots," menaced Rachel B. "You each have four things to learn, and they're all going to take at least a minute to master."

Fifteen minutes later, the trio were old pros. 1) Throw ideally-but-not-necessarily-thawed-out patty on grill. 2) Wait one minute. 3) Flip burger patty. 4) Place patty on bun. There was that wicked twist, the one where some burgers got cheese placed on them, after step 3), but some did not. That part was totally confusing. Gideon decided that if they were wrong in the over-cheesing direction, they'd be gold. He told the other two, that, when in doubt, slap on the cheese. It wasn't like anyone could *taste* the crap. Its only function was to be orange.

Zebah was working the counter. Gerald gleaned, instinctively, that she was a people-person, at least as it came to male people.

Rigel was appointed pearl-diver first class. That really excited him. So far, while washing and scrubbing pots and utensil, he'd not found a single pearl. But, as always, he was optimistic, and plied himself to the task with near-abandon.

Gideon was a burger wrangler. His duties did not, as of yet, extend to bun-dresser, or wrap-it-up-dude. That was fine with him. Gideon was going to space out and hardly be productive. Burger wrangler fit his expectation the best of any job at the dump.

After twenty minutes of flipping, cheesing, and slinging, Gideon noticed a large rat standing by his side. He jumped away, only to find it was Gerald, studying him closely.

"There a problem, here, kid?"

"I told you twice already. Do not call me kid, pops. I'm, not a kid. I'm a young adult."

"What, you about eleven? That qualify *anywhere* as a young adult?" He huffed, for emphasis.

"I'm eighteen and three quarters, for your 4-1-1. I've worked here since I was seventeen." Gerald held up five fingers. "That's *four* years, pops. Count'em."

"If I were any more impressed, I'd fall asleep standing."

"Oh, yeah. What's that supposed to mean, gramps?"

"It means you're a dick, sonny boy. Now," he gestured to the grill, "actually working, here. Can you go rot away in some other space, besides any space that includes me?"

"Is that how you talk to your immediate *supervisor*, old gramps?"

"Let me see. Hang on, I know you're otherwise not busy. Hmm. *You're a dick, sonny boy. Now, actually working, here. Can you go rot away in some other space, besides any space that includes me?* Yup, that's pretty much how I talk to my immediate stupidvisor."

"Hey, don't *call* me that. Did Phil from fries tell you to call me that like he does?"

Gideon was dumbstruck. "Kid, everyone, everywhere knows that barb. What planet are you from?"

"*Earth*," Gerald returned angrily.

"Ah, that explains it."

"What I'm here to discuss with you in a positive, open-ended manner, free from confrontation or ire, is how you are turning the hamburger product."

Gideon held up his spatula. He made flipping motions in the air.

"Not *how* you flip them but *when* you flip them, mucous brain."

"What happened to *positive, open-ended manner, free from confrontation or ire?*"

"That's as much as I remember from the stupid classes they forced me to take after the second and fifth lawsuits."

"Who ever learned anything in a class?" Gideon said, supportively. "Aside from being an excellent venue to hit on babes, what good are classes?"

"Exactly. Stupid classes. And the even stupider community service."

"I hear ya, brother. Cleaning up live drunks and dead skunks. How's that help a man expand his horizons?"

"It doesn't, that's how." Gerald seemed to notice Gideon for the first time, ever. "Say, you're a pretty slick guy."

Gideon nodded to the flattop. "It's the grease, kid. Splatters like lava from a mighty volcano." He reflected for a moment, but only that one. "Say, what kind of meat is this, anyway?" He pointed to a grouping of patties, spurting hot grease.

"Are you kidding me Sideon?"

"*Gideon.* If you forget, you can always read the name tag." Gideon gestured to his with his new favorite toy—his *man*-spatula.

Reflexively, Gerald eyed Gideon's name tag. It read *I Can't Remember, Either.*

"Say, I'm not certain that's regulation, per specified corporate directives clearly spelled out—"

Gerald stopped whining, which is to say speaking, when he heard Gideon begin to snore. In his defense, Gideon actually was asleep. Mention *corporate* anything, and he relapsed into narcolepsy. Gideon was quickly awakened when a particularly large splat of grease landed on Gerald's cheek. He squealed like a little girl, and that brought Gideon back to the here and now, unpleasantly.

"So, you were saying what kind of roadkill this is."

"That, pops, is ninety-seven percent USDA inspected beef."

"What's the other three percent?"

"Three percent of what?"

"That," Gideon pointed with his man-spatula, "is one hundred percent *something*. You said it's ninety-seven percent beef. *Ergo*, what is the other three percent?"

"Nothing. In my assistant manager orientation class, they specified that the jewel in our crown, so to speak, was one-hundred percent, ninety-seven percent beef."

"That still begs the question as to what the mysterious other three percent is composed of."

"Oh, I see your issue. The instructor told the girl who asked that in class to leave immediately. Then she asked the class if anyone else felt the need to ask the same question."

"And no one said a peep," Gideon responded, judgmentally.

"That's where you're wrong. A man with a funny accent and the woman who turned out to be an undercover FDA inspector asked the same thing."

"And?"

"And what?"

"What happened to them?"

"Are you asking me?"

"No, the platypus standing behind you, the one with the cheap toupee."

Gerald turned. "You were asking me, weren't you?"

"Clever boy."

"Well, the man who talked funny disappeared. No one saw him, after class, or anything."

"And the inspector, she sort of disappeared, too."

"No, the teacher, she got real mad. She grabbed the inspector by the scruff of her neck and frog-marched her out of the room. The teacher kept yelling at her. She was real mad. She was real strong, too, it turned out."

"What was the instructor yelling?"

"So, you want to see what the other three percent is? Well, you're going to find out, up close and personal."

"Oh, my. That's harsh, even by my lax standards."

"What is?"

"Grinding the inspector up into ... into—" Gideon finally just angled his man-spatula at the same grouping of patties.

One-two-three-four, and because Gerald was just that dense, five-six-seven ... "Oh, my golly. You don't think ... you aren't saying ... I cannot believe the teacher would do that."

"Desperate people do desperate things, in my experience."

"She actually took the inspector to the plant and showed her the entire process and allowed her unfettered access to all products and equipment used in the fabrication of the jewel in our company crown?"

"Sure. What you said."

"I guess the *inspector* knows what that unaccounted for three percent of our jewel in the crown product is?"

"Indeed she does. Up close and personal."

"Say, do you think those patties have been broiled for a period in excess of the corporately specified thirty seconds on that side?"

Gerald pointed to the same, black-on-one-side-raw-on-the-other-side burgers.

"You know, it's hard to say. Do you think I should flip them, yet? I mean, we should really cook them well. The human mouth is supposed to be a cesspool of nasty bacteria."

"Hey, Bideon, once the customer takes that first bite, it's their problem what's in their mouth."

"Kid, you're like an oracle or a prophet or something. Wise beyond your years, I say."

"I ... I think it's time to flip them."

"You're the boss," Gideon replied, as he began using his man-spatula for the purpose it was made.

"Which ones get cheese?"

"I give up. Which ones get cheese?" Gideon replied, deadpan.

"That descriptor appears on the comput ..." Gerald looked around quickly. "Where's the computer unit for this designated work station?"

"Computer? I don't believe I saw a computer when I came on duty."

"What do you mean, you didn't see one? When I gave you your brief but comprehensive in-servicing on this duty station, it was right here." Gerald gestured to where a platform of metal had been neatly cut off, almost as if whoever did the dirty work had access to a powerful laser beam.

"Are you certain?"

"Of course, I'm certain, pops. I've been—"

"Working here since you were seventeen. I recall that factoid. I'm sure your parents are supremely proud of you."

Gerald looked nonplussed. "You really think so?"

"I'd bet my entire life savings on it, kid."

"So when they scream at me that I'm almost as great a failure as I am a disappointment to them, they're not being totally honest?"

"It's called *Tough Love*. It's their way of encouraging you to excel."

"It is?"

"Look where it's got you." Gideon quipped, scanning burger central.

"I guess I never thought of it like that."

"You never met me, kid," Gideon boasted.

"No. I do not believe I had, until today, Lideon."

Gideon tapped his name tag with his man-spatula.

"Sorry, Mr. Either."

"Consider it forgotten."

There was a blessed silence, as Gideon reckoned. Then the assistant shift manager spoke, or rather whined, again. "That brings me back to which sandwiches get cheese and where is the computer that services this station?"

"Gerald, for the love of God, no. You can't put computer parts on these taste treats. You'll *kill* someone."

"No, I said cheese for the sandwiches. Computer parts would be cost-saving, but unwise, in the big picture, long term."

"If you say so. You are the boss, Boss. Me, I'm just a run of the mill interstellar hooligan and swashbuckler, par excellence."

"Your application stated you were a past professional *liability*, not a hool ... hool ... wash bucket."

"I'm going to need you to depart my designated work station, in the interest of international safe-food practices."

"Ah, okay." He pointed to the charred remains of nearly pure cow meat. "Do you think those might be—"

Gideon swung his man-spatula like a sword, narrowly missing Gerald's hard-to-miss nose. "Out, damn'd spot! out, I say!"

CHAPTER SIX

Over the next few days, the three travelers,\' lives settled into a comfortable routine. Zebah worked up front and would take orders, for which she received truly spectacular tips. She would also record what the patron wanted to eat and send those request back to the kitchen, if the person *also* wanted food. Rigel was ever more committed to his assignment. By the third day, he'd thought it wise to purchase a mask and snorkel, so he might see the pearls at the bottom of the wash sink. Not having found any yet was not deterring his zeal.

After showing up late, disappearing regularly during his shift, and leaving early, only to return and clock out when he was supposed to get off, insulting all other employees, and producing exclusively inedible meat patties, Gideon was promoted. Gerald named him his associate assistant shift manager. There was no increase in pay (or duties, for that matter), but there was the *power*. Gideon learned, for the first time in his life, that he actually loved power. He came to know what it was to command men, to be adored by women, and to hold in his bare hands the fate of all that he ruled and lorded over. Gideon learned what it was to be feared by an associate assistant shift manager at a burger franchise.

Of course, being the level-headed, well-balanced fellow that he was, you'd hardly notice an outward change in Gideon, or his behavior pattern. He was still, and always would be, good old Gideon.

"You there," Gideon said, as nasally as possible, "what you are doing does not please me."

Zebah searched frantically for something other than condiments or individually packaged plasticware to throw at him. The service counter of a fast foodery was not the castle walls of old, ready to repel goblin hordes. She settled on the heaviest objects at her disposal. Sugary cream-like oil suspensions in thimble-sized containers.

Three or four boinked off Gideon's head and neck. He was, naturally, unharmed. He chuckled to himself. Gideon was actually quite used to that type of abuse from his subjects, or as he so loved to consider them, his *little people.* "I say, female servant, that was uncalled for. I was just doing my job of trying to make the world a better place to live and raise a family."

Mustard packets and a plastic box containing ancient charity candy either struck, or narrowly missed, the stalwart associate assistant shift manager.

"You know you must pick all those items up, in addition to your wench duties at my service counter."

Zebah couldn't answer his challenge. The small woman was laboring mightily to lift the cash registrar/credit-card-processor unit. Silly of her, if you think about it. If she could barely lift it, how could she logically throw it? But, you have to admire her spunk.

Rigel collided with Gideon, so passionately was he running to speak with him. "Looky, look. I *finally* found a pearl." Rigel held up a chip fragment from a bowl used to mix ice-cream substitute paste prior to its freezing. "How much do you think it's worth, Gideon?"

The associate assistant shift manager frowned the frown only an offended monarch may. "I've told you not to address me, thusly, serf."

"Sorry, Gideon." He took a few calming breaths. "How much do you think it's worth, Noble Associate Assistant Shift Manager, sir?"

Gideon scrunched up his face and studied the shard. "It's worth your life, you lowly fool."

"Really," Rigel wheezed, as he eyed his treasure and assigned it even more value.

"Yes." Gideon slapped it out of Rigel's fingers. "Because, if you don't get back to work, soon and furiously, I'll see you are hanged."

"But my pearl," whined a dejected Rigel.

"It's a piece of *pottery*, knave. It is as worthless as the sum of your existence."

"Are you certain, Gi ... NAASMS?" In the spirit of brevity while working, Gideon had deigned that his little people could shorten his title, if they felt the need to do so.

"That is all I can take. Your rations are halved for a week. Now return to work, lest your back become acquainted with a cat-o'-nine-tails."

"But cats only have *one*, NAASMS."

Gideon began to say something condescending and stupid. But Zebah, plucky Zebah, chose that moment to drop the cash registrar on Gideon's foot. The credit subunit had broken off almost immediately, if you're wondering.

Gideon grabbed his injured leg and began hopping wildly on the other. He screamed in tongues, he was so irate, as he gyrated across the floor. He was so animated, that an elderly Irishman, trying desperately to drink enough coffee to sober up so he could return home that morning and face his shrewish wife, fancied Gideon was dancing a jig. The man cast away his cane and his companion dog's lead, and joined in, riotously. He sang loudly in Gaelic; Gideon, loudly in pain. So impressed were most other patrons that they began clapping in time. It was quite the spectacle, trust me.

As his suffering eased, Gideon took his first note of Donagh McDougall, his dance partner. Gideon came to a full stop, rested his hands on his hips, and protested, "Who the hell are you, and what are you doing?"

"We're dancin', dis fine, fine mornin', lad."

"We are not," Gideon barked.

That was a tactical error, on Gideon's part. Granted, he was likely unaware that Donagh had a high-strung, under-exercised service Doberman Pinscher a few feet away.

The dog's eyes snapped up to Gideon, and it bared its teeth with a bloodcurdling snarl. Gideon didn't see or hear a thing. He was preoccupied with repeating his dressing-down of Donagh, whom he considered defenseless, and safe to abuse. Silly Gideon.

Dìoghaltach flew, in one spring-loaded vault, from under the table Donagh was seated at, all the way to Gideon's buttock. The feat of athleticism was documented from two separate security cameras. It was a breathtaking leap from both vantage points.

Once Gideon's attention was fully captured, he screamed, shook his booty dramatically, and began sprinting from the room. That's when he was reminded of his incapacitated foot, caused by the cash register. The biter and the bitee went down in a furious heap. Growls, cries for salvation, and splats of blood filled the air. In a flash, Gideon was riding Dìoghaltach. In a second flash, Dìoghaltach was riding Gideon.

The two combatants fell apart, Gideon flat onto his back. As he started to rise, Dìoghaltach drew a bead on his throat. Just as death was about to reach out and touch Gideon, Donagh slipped two fingers into his mouth and whistled loudly. His service dog relaxed and trotted over to its master's side.

"I'll have to remember to stop in here after every bender," marveled the elderly Irishman, as he retrieved his cane, and left for his reckoning with the wife. But, he had a smile on his face, and that would surely help with whatever was to come.

Gideon sat up, unsteadily. He scanned the room as if seeing it for the first time, ever. What had just happened, and why did his butt hurt?

Zebah came to his side. "Give me your hand." She helped him to his feet.

"What the heck is going on out here?" whined Gerald. "Does *anyone* know how hard it is for me to fall asleep a second time at work?"

No one replied that they did.

"You, Mideon, I made you my assistant specifically so I didn't have to deal with issues and situations. Don't you remember that part of my instructions to you? Your job is not to manage this dump. Your job is to deflect any issues from reaching *me*."

Gideon was reorienting faster, now. "Good help *is* hard to find."

"Tell me about it. Last week, I actually had to wrap burgers. Imagine that, *me*, having to work right alongside you losers."

"It's unconscionable," mumbled Gideon.

"It's what?" asked Gerald. "Are you mocking me?"

"No, son. You're doing a bang-up job of that, all by yourself."

Gerald grinned. "Do you really mean that? I'm doing a ban ... a ban ... a good job at something?"

"If they gave out awards for witlessness and twaddle, you'd be a shoo-in."

Gerald had no idea what those two attributes were, but he was given great comfort knowing he was finally good at something. *Oh, world*, he shouted in his head, *bite me. You were wrong.*

Poor self-deluded child.

"But, who's going to clean up this mess?"

Gideon looked slowly to the right, and then to the left. "Which one?"

"Do not tell me you don't see a mess, assistant employee," squeaked Gerald.

"No, I don't. I see *multiple* messes in various states of evolution. Which do you think rises to the level of needing to be cleaned up?"

Gerald walked a slow circle around the seating area, hands folded behind his back. His facial expression wavered from serious, to pensive, to that a person without one clue in this life about anything. "None are that critical. But you, as associate assistant shift manager, will need to monitor them all closely. Once a mess reaches the clean-it-or-someone-dies stage, I expect you to hop to it."

"You are as wise as you are unwashed," Gideon praised.

"Thank you associate assistant shift manager. I'll be in my office, if you need me. See to it that you don't."

"You will be unrequired. I guarantee it."

Gideon asked Rigel to stick his head out the entry and make certain the killer dog was gone. Rigel reported that it was. Gideon, was then free to move.

He jumped up on a table, to make an announcement. The table was neither secured to the floor and constructed with heft. It crumbled and skidded out from beneath Gideon.

Zebah gave him a silent applause with the pads of her fingers, and a grin of true appreciation.

Rigel rushed over and helped him up.

Gideon dusted himself off, while recovering his recently lost poise. Then he stood as straight as his bruised back would allow. "Dear valued customers," he began with ample emphasis, "we are staging our annual apocalypse-training drill. Please play along, if you will, since the design of this exercise is to help you, the public, survive a catastrophe well beyond your level of comprehension."

Nervous glances were exchanged with other nervous ones, among the few patrons remaining.

"Thank you. Now, if this had been a *real* end-times scenario, you would be asked to panic. To simulate this initial phase, please scream and strike whomever is to your right. If there in no one to your right, strike the nearest person. After this is accomplished, please loot this sorry excuse for anything at all and run, all the while screaming and striking, into the street. From there, spread the panic as best you can. The drill will only be over when you hear the sound of monkeys dancing on tin rooftops. Are there any questions?"

An elderly woman raised her tripod metal cane in the air, slightly.

"Yes, old person," sang out Gideon.

"I carry this." She rummaged through her rather large handbag, and finally pulled out a Ruger Super Redhawk Alaskan 44 Magnum Stainless Revolver. The poor woman could barely lift it. "Am I free to use this in the simulation?"

"Well, madame, that depends. Is it loaded?"

"Is it loaded? If you think grandma's shooting blanks, so's your pecker." She held it a bit higher. "Frangible loads, sonny."

"In that case, yes, you may use it in our drill."

"Ye ha! Betsy kicks like a son of a bitch, but the girl delivers on every promise she makes."

"On three, people, and make it convincing for the judges. *Three*!"

The room exploded in noise, confusion, and chaos. The old lady, Fannie May Hollister by name, fired off a couple rounds into the ceiling. She was driven to the floor, but with a huge smile on her withered face.

A woman in her middle years picked up a well-dressed man in his early thirties and bolted for the door.

He began screaming, "Oh, no."

She began screaming "Oh, yeah."

Two men ran into the kitchen and came out with a crate each of jewel in the crown frozen burger patties. A group of foreign tourists ripped down all the signage and trademarked materials and dragged them to the bus. The place was ruined in seconds.

Gideon walked quietly but directly out the front door.

Zebah caught up with him, and pulled him to a stop. "What the hell'd you do that for? Kind of hard to work in a place that's in shambles."

"I'm no longer interested in pursuing gainful employment. Certainly not with them. Any company that would not only hire, but retain and promote *me*, promises to be a very bad employer, indeed.

I can't waste my time on endeavors doomed to fail by the weight of their own incompetence."

"OMG," Zebah exclaimed. She stopped and placed both hands on her cheeks.

"What, my dear?"

"I never thought the day would come. You said something thoughtful *and* correct."

"It won't happen again. I promise."

Zebah was about to answer when a small group of rioters zipped past, carrying Rigel. For his part, he was still unaware he'd been co-opted for, no doubt, some nefarious purpose. His face mask and snorkel made seeing anything a challenge, especially above the water surface as he was. Rigel's arms continued to dig deep into the air in front of him, ever hopeful, even when any hope was a thing of the past.

"Should we rescue him?" asked Gideon, studying Rigel's departure.

"Of course we should. He's our *friend,* and he's our *crew* mate," Zebah wheezed.

"I thought you might say something along those lines. Bother."

Gideon trotted after the Rigel-stealing crowd. It didn't take him long to catch up. Seriously, how competent could a group of people be, if they were dumb enough to kidnap Rigel? Yeah, not very.

"Say, could you put my patient down? I think all this bouncing will only serve to shake-loose some of his syphilitic fluids. I don't want other innocents to die in agony, again."

That stopped them. As one, they rotated to face Gideon. So did Rigel, there up-top.

"Are you trying to say this man has *syphilis*?" asked a dimwitted spokesman for the mob.

"No. He doesn't just *have* syphilis. This man is the sole repository for *all* the syphilis there is, anywhere."

Several mob-members exchanged looks of confusion.

"We're not so certain that's even possible, potential liar," responded the same man.

"You know what?" Gideon said, turning away. "This might be just the break we at the institute we're looking for." He nodded vigorously. "Please, keep him. Yes, this works out *perfectly*." Gideon walked quickly away.

The crowd kept pace with Gideon. "Hang on. Why does our keeping him help your institute?"

"Institute? My, whatever are you talking about, stranger?"

"Oh, no. We clearly heard you refer to an institute. Some *syphilis* institute, no doubt, if you ask us."

"I am not—" he began to respond.

"Look, doctor. We're not nearly as stupid as we look. We are, in fact, almost no one's fool. So, be smart and fess up. What's wrong with our sacrific ... *friend*?"

"I've never met the patient."

"Ah ha. So, you admit he's your patient?"

"I can't seem to put anything over on you ... you, whatever you are," Gideon self-chided.

"Who we are is not nearly as important as ... as ... Chasberry, help me out. I'm confused again."

A woman toward the rear of the mob perked up. "Benjo, it's okay. We're not here to judge you. What you meant to say is that who we are is not nearly as important as *what we stand for*."

"Ah," Gideon summarized loudly. "I got it. You know, I stand for several things. Yeah. Royalty. A judge entering a courtroom. Heck, I even stand for passing snakes, if they're tall enough." He gestured an arbitrary height in the air before him. "Yea big and I'm *up* on my feet."

"We're confused," said Benjo. "Are you trying to confuse us, or are you serious?"

78

"*Maybe* I'm seriously trying to confuse you. *Hah*. Have you ever thought about that bitter pill to swallow?"

"Sir, we're beginning to feel you may not be mentally, er, stable."

"Me? Thanks for asking. Fine. Couldn't be ... what was your question?"

"It was more a statement than a query. We think you're bonkers. Insane. No esta aqui en la cabeza."

"No. It's just, as this former human's doctor, I've been exposed to his disease, so, in this case, I've got it, too."

"I thought you said he has all there *is*?" challenged Benjo.

"What would I know. My brain's moldy Swiss cheese, due to my affliction. Suit yourselves."

The crowd looked again amongst themselves.

Abruptly, they dumped Rigel, and scurried off together, like they were stapled together, which, in fact, they were.

"Thanks, Gid," declared Rigel. "Man, I thought I was a-goner there. Do you know what those *lunatics* were about to do to me?"

"No. They didn't say."

"Well, they—"

"Not *interested*, either. Look, we need to go."

"Go where?" he wheezed in frustration. "You just apocalypsed our workplace."

"We're going somewhere else. Somewhere, *new*."

"That *was* new. We worked, we got paid, and we ate every day."

"That's just my point; it *was* new. Then, it became *old*. Old is bad. Off we go." Gideon walked ahead.

"What's the plan?" Rigel called after him.

Zebah hooked her arm into his. "Yeah, fearless leader. What's the plan?"

"Bigger and better?"

"That sounds delicious," she returned.

"It will be. It will be a massive chocolate sundae plan of delicious."

"Any clues?"

"Do I have any, or will I give you any?"

"You choose."

"No."

"Much as I suspected."

"I'm so happy to not disappoint," Gideon said with genuine pride. "I can tell you this, however. Our next undertaking will be unlike those we've pursued to date on planet Earth."

"Oh?" she cooed.

"This is going to be *big*."

She snuggled closer. "I like big."

Gideon pulled away, slightly. "I *asked* you not to remind me of that fact."

Zebah said nothing, but did roll her eyes.

CHAPTER SEVEN

"Look, pal, this'll go a hell of a lot easier if you stop talking crazy and answer our questions as if you were not seriously deranged." Detective Philip Hall was getting frustrated. The last time the detective got this frustrated, the individual being questioned *accidentally* fractured several bones in a bathroom incident. Three months of administrative leave and a letter in his file was what Philip received for what he kept insisting was a freak misfortune. Who knew bathroom stall doors could open and close on their own, so forcefully and so repeatedly?

Swobo Grabski dug his fingers into the metal table so hard, he dented the defenseless piece of furniture. "I told you the plain and simple truth. If you want me to lie, so you feel better about yourself, say the words and I will."

Philip studied the papers he held in his hands. "Tell me about the people you were caught chasing, the ones riding the burros."

"They are aliens. I keep telling you, but you won't listen."

"So, the things that looked like everyday pack animals were actually *aliens*?" queried Officer Patricia Nelt. She was studying to be a detective, and in a small city like this, was able to participate in the questioning of such suspects. As a semi-professional cage fighter, she was also no one to trifle with. The woman all but wore a *No Trifling* sign around her neck.

"No, the stupid animals weren't the aliens, you idiot. The people *riding* them were."

Patricia quietly tallied another mark on the otherwise blank sheet of paper before her on the table. She didn't want to forget any of the many insults, slights, and derision Swobo had heaped upon her. Patricia had a private saying. *Payback's a bitch, and so am I.* Not terribly catchy or flattering, but she reflected on it often, nonetheless.

"The *people* were aliens?" asked the detective. "Aren't—and please correct me if I'm wrong here—aren't *people* sort of by definition *not* aliens? Aren't *people* humans?"

"You're as dull as she is, aren't you?" spat Swobo.

Philip tallied up another tick mark. When you hear someone say, *Who's counting*, think of Phil and Pat. They most assuredly did.

"I saw the videos," stated Patricia. "Two arms, two legs, one head. They sure appeared human to me."

"The female was actually kind of cute," added Phil, with a naughty glance at Pat.

"Don't go there, again, detective. Hmm?"

She was right. After eight failed marriages, a failed affair with Patricia, *twice*, and seventeen—count 'em, seventeen—sexual harassment lawsuits pending, he really should not be commenting along those lines.

"You're speaking about the woman I love," hissed Swobo.

"How does that claim square with the fact that you were running after her with two raised machetes? Is that how aliens *do* it?" He snickered most unprofessionally as soon as he'd said the words.

"No, you *smeroff*," bellowed Swobo. "I'll kill you for those words. No one lives who makes light of my true love, or my true love."

"Sorry, did you just stutter there?" Patricia snickered.

"No, *smeroff dra*. I spoke *of* my true love, Hephzibah, and my true love *for* her. For an *apparent* female, you seem to lack the gene for romantic thought."

Another check mark hit her page.

"So, you love this humalien. Why were you trying to dismember her?" asked Philip. "She two-time you with those other guys. Hmm? Maybe she *two-timed* them, if you know what I mean." More of the snickering. Seriously, such a teenager at heart.

"What's a humalien?" asked Swobo.

"A *human* who you think is an *alien*."

"They *are* aliens. *I'm* an alien," he screamed.

"You know, you really should limit the number of times you howl that. It kind of strengthens the case that you're loony-toons."

"I'm from the planet Fetolz. I'm not human," screamed Swobo.

"Fetolz? Is that Fetolz with an *F*?"

"No, it's not Fetolz with an F, fool. *Sepac - del - tot - cict - umb - het, Fetolz*. Don't they teach human police pigs *anything*?"

Phil didn't catch the spelling. He was busy recording another reminder.

"Look, Simba, we found blood on those pig-stickers of yours. Once we identify the source, you're looking at hard time—hard prison time."

"Swobo. How many times do I have to tell you my name's *Swobo*?"

"I never heard that name. What kind of name is it?" he asked suspiciously.

"*Alien*," seethed Swobo.

"Are we back to that?" asked Pat. "When our lab proves the blood on your weapons is blood, you're going down. Do you know what they do to chubby boys like you in prison, Swimboy?"

"Swobo."

"I *think* I'll let that be a surprise for you. Yeah. *Spoilers*," she taunted.

"If you're an alien, where's your spaceship?" challenged Phil, getting back to serious-lite.

"Such an idiot. Not all aliens have spaceships." Swobo tried to calm himself. "Do you know how much a spaceship costs?"

"Not offhand," he replied, glancing up to Pat. Then he snickered.

"Anything worth risking your life in costs *thousands* of zettles."

"Zettles, eh?" he responded, dubiously. "A zettle, that's a lot of money?"

"Yes. It's worth, oh, I don't know, about one *zettle*, you prax-dancer."

Cross the four, makes five. Fifteen total, so far.

"So what, you take the *subway* to Earth, pudgy boy?" pressed Pat.

"Sub-swine unit female, you are as stupid as the man I hunt. There is no *subway* in space. What planet ... Wait. Forget I asked. There's no *sub* to *way* in space. One takes the bus, cow."

Seventeen. Still ahead of Phil, Pat beamed in her head.

"The bus. You mean, like a ... a bus?"

"Yeah. Just like one moronovich," howled Swobo. "Windows, surly drivers who demand exact change... No, pus-brain. They're long spaceships with rows of affordable seating. They make a lot of stops, yes, but they get you from here to there economically enough."

"And there's—" Pat doubled over with a big snicker. "And there's a bus that stops at Earth?"

"Not too many, I'll tell you that for free. Amazingly few travelers are dumb enough to come *here*."

"Just you and the burros?" questioned Philip. Yeah, he snickered but good.

"Why'd you say you wanted to kill this Godfry fellow?"

"Gideon, Gideon, *Gideon*. How many times must I say the defiler's name before your monkey brains retain it?"

"Why, again?" Philip pressed.

"He deserves to die, that's why."

"Makes sense, if you put it that way. I mean, me, looking at him on that vicious alien donkey, I thought he looked a regular enough guy," taunted Phillip. Phil just loved to taunt suspects. Beat them too, but taunting was almost as satisfying.

"Are you mocking me?" seethed Swobo.

"Yes. And I must be doing a pretty damn bad job of it if you feel the need to ask. Look, I'll summarize your statement, so far. Then you tell me who's nut-cakes here. You're Stupid, Fact One. You fell in love with a hooker. You're Stupid, Fact Two. When said sleaze merchant became a zombie, your love only grew. You're Stupid, Fact Three. You blamed the zombie's pimp, not yourself, for keeping you apart. Anyone with eyes could testify that it was *you* who she dumped. You're Stupid, Fact Four. You came to Earth to kill the man who you feel wronged you, via Interspace Greyhound. You're Stupid, Fact Five. You keep *repeating* the first four facts. Swombo, you're stupid."

"Fine. My name's Mervin Winklegfat, from Peoria. I don't get out much, so I like to mass-murder whenever I do. The woman was the first one I'd seen in months, so I chose to stalk her and her husband and brother. There, are you happy?"

"Absolutely. Now we're getting somewhere. Now, when you say brother, is it her brother, or the husband's?" Philip tried to clarify.

"Oh, *that* story you swallow," protested Swobo. "You're both such *ucelfubs*."

They exchanged unknowing glances, then, in the interest of completeness, marked that on their respective tallies.

"Okay, Swomble, I think I have enough here to ask the DA for an indictment," Phil said, as he scribbled a few things down. "Now we just need to take a bathroom break, and we can book you into—"

"I don't need to use the restroom," Swobo protested, absently.

"Good, less messy that way. When accident victims are rendered unconscious, the bowels have a nasty tendency to empty themselves." Philip knew of what he spoke, in spite of having no formal medical training.

"Whoa, bucko. If his accident's going to be that severe, I think *I* need to take him on his bathroom break, first. I'm not letting you leave me at the altar, again."

"You're taking me to the women's room?" wheezed Swobo. "That's ... that's—" He couldn't find the words.

"Oh, no. You pig," Pat snapped back. "That's so gross. You just gave me gooseflesh. She pointed to her forearm with her pencil.

Swobo checked, but couldn't make out any feathers.

"I'm taking you to a gender-*neutral* personal hygiene station for your acci ... *convenience*."

"Why do you both keep talking about my impending accident? I'll have you know I've used the potty now for three hundred years and never had an accident while doing so."

Both officers held up their tally sheets, to demonstrate how they knew he was about to meet with ill-fortune.

"I demand you release me."

"Well, if you're such an alien, why don't you use your *laser* eyes to cut the handcuffs off and then escape?" challenged Pat.

"Do you have any idea how much laser eyes cost?" spat Swobo. "I'm a humble man. I can't afford those."

Patricia held up her arms to Philip. "We're going to *have* to request a psych eval, Phil. There's no getting around it here."

"I know, I know. But not until after his accidents."

"Phil, the last time we agreed to wait until after, the perp saw an *actual* doctor for his psychiatric evaluation. We nearly got outed."

"Yeah, I guess the psychiatrist not being able to speak a word of English *was* a lucky break. He was suspicious, but, with only us to ask for details, he was kind of hamstrung."

"So, what's it going to be? One relatively minor accident in the gender-neutral john, or you, who always looses control when the drooling begins?"

"*Damn* the drooling. It *so* gets me going," Philip lamented. He started shadow boxing.

"Okay, Slubo," declared Pat, "This is your last chance to disappear like an alien. Otherwise, you need to go to the bathroom."

"If I disappear, how's that help?" He strained to demonstrate the cuff that were interlaced with the chair. "I'm still stuck here."

"Oh, so if we only removed the cuffs, you could slip from our grasp, and keep your date with blunt-force trauma?" asked Phil.

"Sure. You knew that, right?"

"'Course we did. You said it yourself. You're from Fetolz with a *Sepac*."

"So you'll take them off?" Swobo asked, with hope mixed with incredulity.

"Only because you're not our first prisoner from Fetolz with a *Sepac,* chum," replied Pat, as she unlocked the cuffs.

"So—" Philip began to say.

Swobo disappeared, suddenly.

Philip looked to Pat, then back to where the perp had been seated.

"That was fresh," he observed.

"What was fresh?" responded Pat, tearing off her tally sheet and crumpling the paper up. Then she popped the wad into her mouth. A lot of stuff when into Pat's mouth, it turned out.

"The Swimbo du—" Then he realized he was advocating for his reprimand, based on the loss of *another* detainee. "Where's lunch?" he asked with disinterest.

"I don't know. I'm in the mood for something *different*."

"You mean alien?" he responded, perking up considerably.

"You still have that suit, the one with the helmet?"

"And *all* that *Velcro*," Phil replied with a lascivious grin.

"Me first," she squealed ebulliently.

That was just like Pat and Phil. When confronted with lemons, make   twisted   lemonade.

CHAPTER EIGHT

Zebah, a heavy sleeper ever since her zombie days, stirred. There was a rustling in the closet. Then a banging. Then a thud, and a muffled curse. She drifted back to sleep, but sat up when she heard the sounds of a landslide, or avalanche, coming from the closet. She got up, slipped her feet into her cushies, and went to investigate.

She poked her head in.

"Help," came a crushed voice, from under a pile of junk.

Zebah found a broom and used it to push the upper debris away. After a bit of effort, she found a hand. Following it to its source, she found Gideon's face.

"Good morning," he said, cheerily enough.

"It was up until this inexplicable moment," she grumbled.

"It is from my perspective," he opined. "It's not every morning you look up to see an upside-down naked woman in slippers straddling you."

Zebah had to think back on that one. "No," she finally agreed, "not that many mornings, at all."

She grabbed his exposed hand, and helped pull him free of his entombment.

"Thanks, really."

"What were you doing under there?"

"Ah, being crushed."

"No, I mean, what were you doing such that you were crushed by all that crap you insist on hoarding?"

"It's called saving for a rainy day, and I was looking for something."

"*No*," she feigned surprise. She reached up and pulled one of her robes from its hanger.

"Must you?" Gideon asked, encouragingly.

"Oh, I *must*," she replied, as she threw it on. "If I reward this behavior, whatever it is, you'll pull the same crap every morning until I put my foot down."

He smiled so joyously he nearly exploded. "Would you put your foot down, really?"

"I hate you," she declared as she left the confines of the closet.

"I was trying to find my hiking boots," he said as he followed her out.

Zebah sat at her vanity. "*You* were going for a hike?"

"Yes. Why do you ask so ... so dubiously?"

"You're not the outdoorsy type."

"I know. That's because I can't find my hiking boots."

"No," she responded forcefully, angling her head. "You can't *find* them because you never *use* them, because you're not the outdoorsy *type*."

"I'm glad you perceive my dilemma."

"I perceive your *dementia*."

"So you haven't seen them?"

"The boots?"

Ne nodded encouragingly.

"Did you ever *have* a pair?" she asked, straining her voice, slightly.

"Not that I recall."

"Then how could you be looking for them? That's bass-ackwards."

"I said I couldn't *recall* owning a pair. I had to look, because I needed some hiking boots."

She rolled her eyes and, yet again, cursed her fate. "Why did you need them?"

"Why? Because today I'm going on a long walk, a hike."

"This dawn does bring nothing but new surprises. We're taking a hike?"

"You and Rige can come if you want. I, however, *need* to."

"Take a hike?" she asked most skeptically.

"Or a long walk. I can't be certain as of yet."

"Of course not. How could you know where you're going?"

"Thank you." He kissed her forehead, gently.

She slapped him across the face. He had, you see, or probably didn't see, at the same time slipped his ice-cold hand up her short robe. He was ever the optimist. You had to credit him for that pluckiness, that willingness to go the extra mile.

"Why," she asked, as he rubbed his cheek, "do you, of all people, need to go on a hike?"

"Or long walk."

"Or long walk."

"Because, there are no high cliffs above rugged rocks, or pits of burning ash nearby."

There were, in fact, none.

"High cliffs? You want to *climb* high cliffs? Scale them, ascend them?"

"How else would I get to their tops? They don't have elevators, now do they?"

"Not to the best of my knowledge," she replied honestly.

"No, silly. They don't."

"And you wish to scale high cliffs over perilous bases because—"

"Well, I suppose a tall bridge would do. Or building. But they'd have to be dramatically tall, and preferably picturesque."

"Picturesque?"

"Well, yes. Call me a hopeless romantic."

"You're suddenly a romantic? You're lustful to a fault. Sex crazed to a deranged-adolescent's extent. But romantic? No. Believe me, I would know."

"I'm glad that you do. That will give me great comfort ... *after*."

90

"After?"

"Yes. Well, okay, before, too. But it's the *after* where it really kicks in." He placed a palm over his heart.

"Gideon Prime," she asked, fully frustrated, "why do you need to hike, or a long-walk, to a dangerously high location, this morning?"

"Or a location that's *sort* of high, over a *dangerous* base," he corrected helpfully.

"Got you. Why?"

"How else can I assure myself of a successful suicide?"

"Um, let's see. You could keep stringing me along, and I'll slay you where you stand, you bastard."

"Ah," he raised a finger, "But that would be murder, not suicide."

"It would be more *certain*, I can assure you of that before the fact."

"You've always been so kind to me. Always." He placed his palm back over his heart.

She snatched his hand and threw it toward the floor. To her disappointment, it remained attached and didn't bounce wetly off the hardwood. "Why do you wish to kill yourself, violently, I might add, this morning?"

"Are you seriously asking? I ... I thought you *knew*?"

"If I knew, I wouldn't ask, now would I?"

"Let me get back to you on that."

"Not a problem."

"Thank you."

"You're welcome." She blinked first. Zebah balled up her fists, stomped the floor with one foot, and screamed, "Why are you in the mood to off yourself? Tell me or *die*."

"Thank you, again, for your kind, time saving offer. But no thank you. I need to do this myself."

She was done speaking. She crossed her arms ... and waited.

"It's just that I've had such a bad run of luck lately," he said with a boo-hoo face to beat even a dejected, emotionally wounded toddler's version of a similar expression.

"You call last-night-into-early-this-morning *unlucky*? Very few men would be so foolish as to say those words."

Gideon reflected, but did not give voice to the thought, that most *women* would be foolish to say so, either, given the facts.

"I just have a hard time living with myself."

"Gid, we all have a hard time living with you. Nothing's changed. That's *never* going to change."

"Thank you, bless you, kind Hephzibah."

"Screw yourself and your next of kin."

"My recent run of unsuccessful investment interventions has led me to a very dark, self-doubting place. I cannot go on."

"Does that include the *Gid-e-on got swin-dled* thing?" she just had to ask, by way of kicking a dog while it was down.

"Most pointedly."

"Honey, not to put too much effort into the saving your life thing, but we've had runs of luck much worse than this one. Lots worse."

He perked up. "Really? Name one."

She felt instant regret. "Hmm. There was the time ... no, that was someone else." She tapped her chin. "What about when you tried to counterfeit Youclipsian currency? That ended horrifically."

"Who knew that some live currencies could be so vicious?" he reinforced.

"Hey, there was the time you proposed to me. You really pressured me on the issue, too. Remember?"

"Yes. I was, I believe, in the middle. You were both on top *and* underneath, at the time."

"Bingo. *That* ended poorly."

"It did?" He thought back on the occasion.

"Remember how upset the doctor was who had to cancel his sex counseling-session with me because he needed to work late patching you up?"

"Ooh," Gideon grimaced. "He was rather vengeful, wasn't he? Like it was *my* fault."

"He was *as* shallow as he was good looking."

"You're not actually making me feel *better* about my self, you know?"

"I'm sorry. I'll try harder."

He was about to thank her, when it struck him she might not have been acting kindly to him, there in the hour of his passion.

"So, when are you leaving?" she asked as she scratched absently at her hip.

"The sooner the better."

"Shouldn't that be my line?"

"You're welcome to it, once I'm ... gone."

"Gone, as in left here *gone*, or do I have to wait until you're *gone* as in dead and *gone*?"

"You choose."

"What time will you be back for lunch?"

"Oh, not too very late. I'd hate to spoil taco Tuesday for the rest of you."

"You should get one of those humanitarian awards I hear so much about."

He swelled. "You think so?"

"No. I very much don't."

"Ah, well, none of that life-stuff really matters to me ... anymore."

"Gideon, get over yourself hasto *prontimediately*. You get nicked, for once. Big deal. You don't make it in the burger corporation. That's a blessing, says I. You're having a hard time figuring how to get an angle on a fat patsy. You'll figure it out. You work spontaneous, spur of the moment kind of deals the best. You've never been good at the sting, or long term scam. Slam, bam, thank you, ma'am. That's my Gideon."

"I like the way you say slam, bam, thank you, Zebah."

"I said *ma'am*, generically, not *my* name."

"Are you certain?"

"Positively so."

I'm sure I heard Gideon-do-you-want-to-slam-bam-thank-you-Zebah-me-right-here-right-now."

"I'm certain that is what you heard. But it is neither what I said nor meant to imply."

"Not even to stop me from making the biggest mistake of my life?"

"Are we back to the topic of you committing suicide, again?"

"Heavens no. I'm talking about me not having sex, immediately."

"How is you not having sex with me immediately the biggest mistake of your life?"

He dropped to his knees. "Because, if you don't, I'll kill myself. And that would be a mistake."

"Because—"

"If I did, I couldn't jump your bones immediately after, you know, the slammy thing you got me going with in the first place."

"That's circular reasoning at its worst, Gideon."

"You see what you've done to me, already. I'm putty in your hands."

"No, you're putty in your *brains*."

Rigel entered the bedroom. He'd heard the heated discussion/angst. "Hey, guys. What's going on?"

Zebah turned to him, disgusted. "What time of day is it?"

"Ah, he wants sex, again."

"Bingo-matic."

"I feel your pain, sister," Rigel responded.

"Oh, but if you could?" she said walking away.

"Could he?" Gideon wondered out loud.

Rigel ran to put Zebah between him and Gideon. It was more a precaution than an act of fear.

In the kitchen, minutes later, when only Gideon was still fixated on carnal issues, they drank coffee in quiet.

"I do declare," Gideon began, "the only thing of any value on this rock is coffee. Why have they got it, and the rest of us—"

Huh?" throated Rigel. "The rest of us what?"

"Back away, slowly," warned Zebah.

"Wh—"

"I said, back away slowly. Do it *now*," she hissed.

When they were ten feet from the table, and Gideon, Zebah spoke, barely above a whisper. "He's lost in scheming."

"He *is*?" marveled Rigel.

"Yes. And he could go off at any moment. Any—"

"I've *GOT* it!" screamed Gideon.

A picture fell off the wall, and the neighbor's cat affixed itself to the ceiling, the sound was so intense.

"We'll sell coffee to the rest of the galaxy. We'll make moola, money, coin, bank, scratch, money."

"You said *money* twice," observed Zebah.

"I know. That's how much we'll make. We'll need to say the word over, and over, and over again."

"Gideon, seriously. There are several aspects of your scheme that are obviously questionable. First, the Norfimdians are in the crop-circle coffee business already. Piss them off, and they'll eat you, then put whatever comes out in prison for a very long time."

"I'm not going to impinge on their turf one tiny bit." Gideon had "That Look" in his eyes. Zebah hated "That Look." It always meant trouble.

"Okay, plus, running an export business is real work. There're employees, bribes, buyers to line up and keep happy. And no, I'm not doing that again, so don't ask." Zebah was firm on that point.

His arms spread in protest. "Who knew Saucians oozed that much when their passions brimmed?"

"Everyone."

"Not to worry. I said I wanted to *sell* coffee to the galaxy. I have, however, no interest in *delivering* coffee to the galaxy. What do I look like, a *newspaper* boy?"

"I should *be* so lucky," replied Zebah, with a heavy sigh.

"Oh, you mean—" Rigel stopped mid-sentence. "But, if you *sold* a product you never intended to *deliver*, wouldn't that be illegal? Also, isn't it dishonest and dishonorable?"

"I certainly hope it's illegal. How else could the profit margin be so seller-friendly? But," and Gideon was thunderously serious, "do not ever say my life's work is dishonorable. I'll strike you if you do. I'm a crook, to be certain. I'm as dishonest as eternity is long. But *honor*, my good fell—"

Gideon stopped speaking when a heavy pair of hiking boots struck, and lodged in, his mouth.

"Hey," exclaimed Zebah, "guess what I found?"

The first step in any respectable scam is to select your target audience; that is, the mark or marks. Ideally, they would be hopeful individuals who suffer under the burden of also being dumb. However, if you're aiming high, as Gideon tended to do, they need lots of money to fleece. Financially hopeful, yet dumb combined with rich; now there's a select group. Where are they? The children of the ultra-wealthy? No, those brats had no aspirations or goals other than for their parents to die. Their only hope was to access the family's fortune sooner than mom and dad's current health predicted was likely.

No, the key, as Gideon saw it, was that the vast sums of money need not belong to the individual being plucked like a chicken. Who were they? You got it. Those who labor on behalf of you and me as public servants. Limited salaries and prospects, fingers on the control switches for oodles of money, and dumb enough, let's face it, to become public employees. (After all, government work is the last refuge of the incompetent.) Their mothers told them to study hard and become doctors, lawyers, or financiers. They chose security with a pension, good dental coverage, and a devastatingly bleak work environment.

But few public employees have unfettered access to large pools of idle cash. Which are the chosen, the floodgate controllers? Of course, the politicians. Which are the easiest to sway, to dangle a too-good-to-be-true carrot in front of? You got it (say, you're perhaps a bit too good at this), the ones who are failing to advance, those stuck in absurdly low positions that enjoy the public trust. Ones who have failed to scale the ladder of success to positions of increasing power, where they too can have mistresses with ever-increasing breast sizes and ever-diminishing standards. Yes, find yourself a political hack lolling in a mid-level capacity with a campaign fund so emaciated they are guaranteed career and extramarital stagnation, and you've found yourself a mark of distinction, a rube to treasure as much as the monies he controls.

What, you ask perceptively, if the politician you are considering is a woman, and almost certainly immune to the larger-breast, non-existent standards, extramarital thing? Run. Leave her alone. She'll take a meeting with you only after she's contacted the authorities and the casual dining restaurant you pitch her in will be secured and monitored better than the Crown Jewels. No, as with so many aspects of adult life, you need to acknowledge and *work* with reality, not foolishly attempt to bend it to your perceptions. People who do that are called *idealists*, which doesn't, but should, rhyme with the word *disappointed*. In other words we're talking about good old Mom here. Do not try to con Mother. Just don't. You'll get pie, weak, lukewarm tea, unconditional empathy, but not one red cent. *No, you're better than that*, she'd coo. And you'd believe her, if only for a while.

Where, oh where, was Gideon to begin? He needed A) A credible source who believed that Gideon was going to make repeated, significant purchases; B) The aforementioned foundering political hack, C) In the best case, a potential spoiler. That person would threaten to buy whatever Gideon was hustling, therein excluding the hopeful but dumb mark. Any respectable three-card monte con, for example, needs a shill; and, finally, D) Seed money. The mark would need to be wined-and-dined, shown fabulous homes overflowing with bikini-clad girls. (Unless the target was not humanoid. Then the scantily clad girls might be misinterpreted as potential snacks. Nothing good could come from that turn of events.)

Where was there a planet whose society was stuffed full of public employees, all wishing they had a chance at fortune? It had to be a relatively rich planet. Lots of worlds were fairly well-off. But abundant funds often meant a large military was possibly associated with the government. Large militaries were not desirable for Gideon. Vindictive, swindled people with abundant lethal weapons were a bad fate to tempt.

Gideon sat in front of his ship's computer, browsing a list of possible candidates the AI had compiled. Twenty five reasonable choices were selected. That was promising. Gideon was in the process of outlining each planet's pros and cons, when Rigel walked up behind him.

"What ch'doing?" he asked, in an upbeat tone.

"Buying you a burial plot, online," Gideon replied matter-of-factly.

"Really?" Rigel responded, surprise evident in his words.

"Sure. I knew you were going to come over here and bug the crap out of me. When you did, I'll need and want to kill you. Once that was in the books, bingo," he gestured to the screen, "a respectful yet affordable site to dump your useless body would be required."

It took Rigel a few seconds, but he realized, or rather hoped *severely*, that Gideon was kidding around. "Ah, you don't want to be disturbed, is that it?"

"No, Disturb ahead. Say, would you mind terribly if I interred you on Vaperon 8?"

"Vaperon 8? Isn't that a gas giant way way out at the periphery?"

"Excellent Trivial Pursuit knowledge there, Rige. It is."

"How can a body be buried on a planet with no dirt, or even rock?"

"I orbit the planet, open the hatch, and gently shove your casket toward the center of the planet."

"Wh ... wh ... what if you missed? Any moving body ... I mean object, is likely to enter an elliptical orbit, not ghost into the gas clouds."

"Not if you leave real quick after doing the deed."

"I ... I fail to see how the length of time the depositing ship remains would have any influence on the chances of the coffin orbiting versus its gradual descent."

"It wouldn't, you silly guy. But if I leave quickly enough, I'll never know. That's as good as knowing the outcome was the one I favored in the first place."

"It is?"

Gideon turned. "It is for me."

"I'm not certain—"

"What? You think it might conceivably matter to you? No way, baby cakes. You'll be dead in less than a minute. Where your remains *remain* is right there beside the other least-of-your-concerns."

"What *is* the least of my concerns, after you kill me and shove me rudely into orbit in the cold of deep space?"

"How should I know? What, am I one of your shrinks, now?"

Rigel thought about that grim prospect long and hard. In fact, he thought so long, and to the exclusion of all other matters that might otherwise occupy a functioning mind, that he forgot what Gideon and he had been discussing.

"What ch'doing?" Rigel asked, in an upbeat tone.

Gideon slumped forward. He'd broken one of his most basic Rigel Rules. He'd engaged the boob in conversation for longer than three sentences. That always went as poorly as a leper's get-away weekend at a whorehouse.

"I'm trying to work here, Rige," he whined in response. "Could you go take a bath while drying your hair—*please*?"

"The last time I tried that, the water must have heated up to fast. I received severe burns on my face and arms."

"And?"

"And what?" Rigel was fairly certain Gideon was getting angry.

"And, you're still alive, right? Your scars are barely visible. Now *scoot*."

"But I want to *help*," Rigel protested childishly.

"Then use two hair dryers."

"I'm serious, Gideon." Rigel stood his ground. If he could only recall on *what* ground he was standing, he'd have felt a lot more certain as to the wisdom of his unexpected spine-growth.

"I'm planning a complex con job. It has to be intricate, predictive of all possible random variables, and, if I do it just poorly enough, we'll all be killed."

"Who will? Are we back to the burial-in-space thing? If we are … well, then I guess we are."

Sometimes Rigel even stunned Gideon with his mental incompetence. It could be … stunning.

"No, we're not. Now go."

"If you tell me what you're doing, and allow me to make suggestions, I'll leave if they're lousy ideas."

"They're lousy ideas. They're so lousy, they died upon contact with the world outside your strange brain. Now leave."

"You haven't heard them to be able to say they're bad ideas."

"I don't need to hear them to know they're stupid, preposterous, and bone-numbingly dull."

Rigel began humming.

"Why are you choking? Not that I mind. I just may want to reproduce the process, soon."

"I'm not leaving until you give me a chance to participate."

"Sure you are. If you don't, I'll toss Mr. Squeaky out an airlock. I swear I'll do it."

"I know your *black* heart, Gideon. It's black. But no heart is able to be so blackly black as to threaten an innocent, not to mention cute-as-a-button, rubber ducky. Not even you."

Damn, Gideon reflected, he was right. What fun would baths be without that yellow saint?

"Okay, you can help. But the instant you say something rigel, you're outta here."

"What do you mean, when I say something I'm out of here?"

"No, when you say something rigel, you must depart. It's an adjective. Rigel, as in lame, anti-clever, something *rigel*."

"You'll see." Rigel sat next to Gideon.

"You bet I will. As soon as you make remark one."

"Where are we, in terms of scheming? I just love scheming."

"We're going to pretend to sell coffee to some as yet undetermined species. I was going over this list," Gideon pointed to the screen, "to see who's the best candidate."

"I like coffee."

"Thanks for sharing. That remark is this close," Gideon pinched his fingers almost together, "to being just rigel enough for me to give you the boot."

Rigel scanned the computer read out. "I'm not familiar with most of those names. Say, I'll bet sense of smell is important, in this setting?"

Without comment, Gideon picked up a fork and impaled the back of his own hand with it. Blood oozed out quickly.

"My goodness. What was that for?" gasped Rigel.

"You ... you said something insightful, relevant."

"Thank you. But why the fork thing?"

"I promised myself long ago that if any words exited your mouth that were not stupid and inane, I'd hurt myself. *Ergo*, the fork thing."

Rigel was determined to prove he was not a one-hit wonder. "Let me see. Excellent sense of smell." He snapped his fingers and pointed at Gideon. "The pelagic trowadons of Vespis are said to have the best olfactory acuity in the galaxy. They can smell *one* drop of blood from ten *thousand* miles away." He nodded, mostly to himself. "That a lot of miles."

"Your point?"

"We could tempt *them* with coffee. With their noses, they'd love it more than any other species."

"You know, that's entirely possible."

"You're welcome," Rigel beamed.

"There's just one, maybe two minor issues."

"Do tell."

"Well, first off, trowadons are gigantic ocean predators. They top-out at three hundred feet long. They have four heads, each with four mouths, each lined with four rows of needle-like teeth. They rip their prey apart, then all the mouths snatch up the pieces. That's it. They don't drink anything other than the blood staining the water. That leads me up to the fact that they don't have tools to make coffee. What they do have, besides an insatiable appetite, are brains the size of ... well, yours, my friend. Finally, if I need to actually say the words, they have no language, culture, or, and this is critical, concept of what money is. If they saw money, they'd eat it. So, it would be very difficult for the tiny chunks of us they *didn't* swallow to turn the necessary *profit* on our scam."

"Do you think so?"

"Kind of certain on this one, big guy. A primitive, rage-driven creature is unlikely to pay good coin of the realm for anything. That brings me around to, that was a very rigel idea. So, Rigel, you are free to get the hell out of my face."

Rigel sat there, very much like a tree stump.

"Are you now deaf, also?" asked Gideon.

"Oh, no. Sorry. Were you speaking to me? I heard Rigel and assumed you were speaking to the adjective, not the person."

Gideon's face pruned up, and steam issued forth from his ears. "Why would I address an adjective, *any* adjective?"

"I give up. Why would you do so?" Rigel trembled, gently. "Is this one of those joke things? I do love a good joke-thing. Knock knock. *Who's there? Adjective. Adjective who?*" Rigel then indicated Gideon should finish the joke.

Instead, Gideon yanked the fork out of his hand, and lowered it toward Rigel's hand. Because anger affected his aim, and since Rigel saw the utensil coming, the fork just nicked the flesh of the target.

"Honestly, Gideon, that's not funny."

"I know. It was a kill shot."

"No, I was referring to the end of your joke. It wasn't funny. Adjective who? Fork a part of you. That makes no ... wait, now I get it. Your response was *fork you*. Ah, very Gideon, if I say so myself."

"Please allow me to repeat myself, over and over again."

Gideon came at Rigel like a deranged sewing machine. Rigel tumbled to the floor, rolled to his feet, and dashed away as quickly as he could.

Gideon smiled. "It worked."

It was time to get back to his planning, now that he was free to think   again.

CHAPTER NINE

Gideon and Rigel sat in the Spartan office of one Glimutive Beta-Thong. Minister B-T, in keeping with the customary shorting of anything felt to be too long on Pejorat 1 (shortened, as it happens, from Perjorat 19, the actual number of the planet circling the star Perjorat. Oh, how Perjorat was diminished by having Pjat-1 associated with it, and hence, the scum on its surface, the Snlv ((shortened form of Snelve)) orbiting its stellar brightness). Rigel wore a suit that telegraphed the notion that it was out of style when it was produced, and that it was purchased at a charity store. The suit said, loudly, *I who wear this am nothing. Never have been, never will be.* Yes, that's a lot for a cheap suit to say, but there you have it.

Gideon dressed in apparent splendor. It was hard, actually, to pin down the fashion endpoint he was expressing, but it did, however, clearly say *I have money.* It said that bold statement because you'd have to be very rich, or very stupid, to wear it. Please note, *stupid* rich people are, functionally, only *rich* people. The stupid part drops off past a certain level of wealth. Gideon's shirt was white fur, from some now furless, involuntary donor. The black tie was dinosaur skin, triceratops, to be specific. The statement there: I don't care if it's ridiculously expensive and critically endangered. I shall wear it if it pleases me. His suit was not silk, but silk*worm.* Tens of thousands of living larvae wriggled and spun, and, at the same time, demonstrated that, while the person wearing them might not have detectable taste, they *did* have immeasurable wealth.

His shoes were not simply alligator skin. They were *live* alligators of a mutant strain evolved solely for the purpose of being worn as dress shoes. Powerfully inappropriate, but that's what someone thought was acceptable. One operational issue a user had to keep always in mind was how to position oneself if one was near another person with similar footwear. Unless due caution was observed, one's right foot could suddenly start mating with the left foot of a perfect stranger.

Gideon, who could never afford such a garish insult to the sartorial world, stole the clothes from a body he had had Rigel exhume. The remains of Doof the Lessless had but briefly rested in the I Had Money Precrematorium and Festive Burial Grounds, before Gideon acquired the outfit. That act, of removing the preposterous clothing from the clueless Lessless, was a kindness to all possible afterlives. They all actually pitched in and sent a card, they were so glad they didn't have to look at the trashy outfit ... forever.

Minter B-T (please note the formal shortening of his title) wore a drab, economically sensible sport coat over pants that didn't match, but were comfortable. He mistakenly felt that made the pairing acceptable. What was left of his thin black tie was only held together by the loose aggregation of food stains and particles that studded it.

B-T was Pjat's High Minister of Fish Money and Brown Morning Beverages. Accordingly, his chair was seventy feet tall. He needed to use an intercom set up to speak casually with any visitors, he was perched up there so high above them. Now, I know what you're thinking. Fish don't have or use money. Right? Wrong. The inhabitants of Pjat -1 used to be fisherman. Like the Portuguese of fifteenth century Earth, they devised an economy based on dry, salted fish. Fish money. While not a single fish survived to *be* money by that period of Pjat-1's dubious history, it was felt to be culturally sensitive to retain the once-important office, if only for sentimental reasons.

Minter B-T's real task in his dull life was to regulate consumable brown morning fluids. Specifically, he was in charge of the planet's tea, hot chocolate, and enjoyed partial control over dark beer. The remainder of brown-beer regulation, and that of any *other* shade of beer fell under the auspice of the Mintry of *Yeah Baby*, which was one floor up. So, as fate would have it, Minter B-T was the perfect patsy for Gideon to swindle. Introducing *the* consumable brown morning fluid—coffee—to a virgin world was going to be big. Er, it *would* be big, if any coffee was actually shipped and distributed. The prospect of really *importing* coffee appeared to be so lucrative, that it caused Gideon to flirt with the crazy notion of returning to Pjat-1 *after* he'd scammed Minter B-T, and becoming an honest merchant. He'd even thought ahead to the extent he decided that if he wore a fake mustache, one of those really big, silly ones, Minter B-T wouldn't recognize him.

"You're so pleased to take this meeting with me, today," began Gideon, in as effete and grating a tone as he could muster.

B-T looked up. "Didn't you mean to say *I'm* so pleased, et cetera, et cetera?"

"I know you are. You're welcome."

"No, I ... forget it." It was going to take too long to explain the damn thing, so B-T let it go.

"What did you say your name was, sir?" queried the minter.

"No, I did not say. I did not say it was *Sir*, sir, either," replied Gideon blandly.

B-T shook his head violently. For the twelfth time that morning he regretted coming to work. "Name?"

"It's on the paperwork, Lord," Rigel responded, groveling right out the gate.

"Who are *you*?" B-T snarled to Rigel.

"I—"

That was all Rigel got out before Gideon thundered, "This man is *nothing*. He is, in fact, less than nothing. If he were *less* nothing, he'd be invisible. When someone said, *hey look over there,* concerning my manservant, you'd look over, but see right through him, because he is invisible nothingness personified. Do I make myself clear?"

"I suppose so," grumbled B-T. "What does he do?" He chuckled quietly to himself. "*Nothing*?"

"No. His soul's sole function is to tell me I'm right. Isn't that right, Oh Nameless One?"

"Yes, sir, Mr. Gideon, sir. You got that right."

"Imagine that," was Gideon's anemic response.

"Wait. Nothingness personified's name is Oh Nameless One? Isn't *that* a name?"

"No, well at least not a very *good* one. No, I should think naming your child *That* would prove to be inadequate, in the long run."

"Naming my child *what* would be inadequate?"

"Yes, *It* would be, too." Gideon tugged at his Moa-leather gloves. "Say, my good man, am I here to help you give pronomial names to your child or am I here to offer you the opportunity of a lifetime?"

"I don't have any children. My wife is barren."

"How dare you, sir," Gideon exploded. "Do not take that tack with me. My wife is a princess. Her brother is a duke. That your wife is a *baron* impresses me not in the least."

"You're right, boss," opined Rigel. "When you're right, you're right."

"Right you are," responded Gideon.

"Are you daft?" howled B-T. "I said my wife was *barren*, incapable of reproduction. Plus, you insensitive lout, if she was a *baron*, she'd be a *baroness*. What planet are you from?"

"Earth."

"Ah," he said nodding gently. "That explains it. My apologies."

"None taken," replied a sullen Gideon.

"Now what's this about offering me the opportunity of a lifetime?" The man hadn't let that slip past, in spite of his indignation.

"It's about time," huffed Gideon. "My name is inconsequential, but it's Gideonvich Nostranonymous."

"Well, which is it? Inconse ... stop. I'm not *saying* any of that. It's too damn long. Is your name insqutl or Gidvch Nsnyms?" He heaved a sigh of relief, relaxed with the shortening of those hideous words.

"It is both, and it's not important."

B-T dropped his heavy head into his waiting, open palms. "This is driving me insane. Now you have another name? That's too many." With resolution comes relief. "Wait. I'll just call you IGNBNI. Man, am I smart or what?" He chanced to look at Rigel.

Rigel pointed to Gideon. "You pay me what he does, and I'll agree. Otherwise, you're on your own, buddy."

"You, sir, are a strange man from a strange land. But, as I can afford to lose no more trillions, I will speak at you, but only just this once."

"Wait, your sitting here," he gestured to here, "has cost you trillions?"

"Yes. I'm so brilliant that I earn trillions per minute. Why, just the other day I took a nap, and an entire *solar* system went bankrupt."

"No way."

"Yes, way," exclaimed Rigel.

"So, here's my proposition," began Gideon. "I have cornered the market for a precious commodity on the planet Earth. It is presently the only world capable of mass producing the blessing of the gods known as coffee." He studied his fingernails. "Have you heard of it?"

"Yes, I have," replied Rigel.

"No, not you." He pointed. "*You.*"

"No, I don't believe I have. What is *coffee*?"

"There is a large distance, sir, between you and adequate intelligence."

"Have you been talking to my mother-in-law?"

"Coffee, my simple friend, in a word, surpasses exquisite."

B-T gestured to Gideon. "Isn't that *two* words, not *a* word?"

"You're likely missing the point here. I can bring the taste sensation of the galaxy here. We—that we is *you* and *I*—can control it from the ground floor, the get-go, the very wellspring."

"If it's all the same to you, I'd rather control it from here," B-T pointed to his office, in general. "I have my stuff here."

"Fine. We shall rule our empire from this roo—"

Gideon's private phone rang with a tasteful chime.

"Yes, hello. Time is money and so am I. Please speak quickly, you've already cost me twenty-five million," he greeted.

Gideon appeared to listen impatiently.

"Of course I remember you Madame Gildefreid ... I mean, Ms. G." Gideon covered the speaker. "I'm so terrible at the sleuth and mouse game."

"You sure are," agreed Rigel. "Terrible. *The* worst."

"Hang on—" B-T began to say.

Gideon raised a scolding digit. "Um, I *must* take this call. I wish to make money, to be certain. But I even more wish to see today's sunset." Directing his attention back to the caller, Gideon listened with wonder and amazement, as if the Oracle of Delphi was on the line. "Yes, those are the *approximate* figures." He studiously listened. "No, sorry, that would be fifty million per *week*, not per *month*. I'm not certain where you got that impression from." More transfixed attention to the caller. Gideon's face contorted, like he was really uncomfortable—his testicles, for example, might have at the juncture been seized by a bear trap. He was a'squirming. "Well, you see, I was just about to seal the deal with—" He looked up to the stunned B-T. "What did you say your name was, again?"

B-T threw his hands up. You see, he'd heard Gideon's misspeak. Ms. G was clearly none other than Mrs. Conrarf Gildefreid, wife, financial backer, and cornhole teammate of the current tyrant running the planetary government. Conrarf Gildefreid was legendary for his cruelty, his unforgiving nature, and his devastating cornhole hooker shot. Mr. G was, however, a pushover compared to his life partner. She was meaner, more impulsive, and if her husband's hooker ever got around her blocker bag —even in a practice round— he would be reacquainted with some serious pain. She was hell on wheels, literally, since she was too ... ah, corpulent (do *not* say large, fat, or blobby within her earshot) to get about easily on her own. To do business with either Gildefreid was a mistake. To even *appear* to cross them in a transaction was lunacy of the first order of magnitude. To be possessed by a death wish was less certain than your fate if you were to anger either of the pair.

"No, no. Don't tell her my name. Our deal is not certain. It's ... why it's not even a deal. I never even met with you."

"You know she can hear you, right?" asked a bemused Gideon.

"No. She cannot, because I'm not here. I was ... never born. Yes, that's it. Now please, whoever you are, leave at once. I'm ... I'm busy not existing."

"Hmm," came dubiously from Gideon's throat. Then the female voice on the other end demanded he return his attention to her. "Ah, I don't know. He said Minter B-T, not his full name." He listened again. "I'll ask. Hang on, don't get gushy on me here."

Gideon covered the receiver and asked, "Is your full name Glimutive Beta-Thong?" He held the phone up. "Lady wants to know."

"W ... why, yes. It is. How could she—"

"Do I look like a lonely heart psychic? I'll ask her, if you don't mind."

He pressed attention, again.

"Wow. That's ... no, calm down. I'll pass that along. Stop ... stop doing that. It's very unsettling."

"What?" gasped B-T.

"She said she recognizes your voice from school. She had the hugest crush on you, but was too shy to reveal her passion."

"Er, we ... I didn't go to school with her."

Gideon lifted the phone again. "He says ... Oh, you heard. Oh. Okay, got it."

"She was so shy no one knew she went to," he snapped his fingers in the air, "what was the name of your school? Belly something, no, nose trail—"

"The *Learning* Academy?"

"That's it. That's the one she mentioned."

B-T was both stunned and impressed. How else could Horsefly have known the name of the tiny school he attended, unless she really did go there too?

"Ah, tell her *hi* from me," B-T said uncertainly.

"He says ... I asked you once not to do that. No, absolutely not. If you take your clothes off, I'm hanging up."

To B-T, Gideon shared, "She keeps making this sucky, gooey sound. Now she says her dormant passion for you is driving her sexually insane." Gideon squinted, "Ah, quick question, if you don't mind. Have you *seen* Ms. G?"

"Well, not lately, not *personally*."

"I'm on record as being glad I'm not you. That's all I can say." Gideon shivered violently.

"What are you suggesting, man?" demanded B-T. "It's not my fault she's madly in love with me. Look at this face. What woman wouldn't be drawn in to this rugged handsomeness? She's only made of flesh and blood."

"Don't know about the blood part, but there sure is a lot of flesh. That much I do recall." Gideon winced, painfully.

"What?" demanded B-T.

"Didn't I hear something to the effect that Mr. G is unbelievable jealous and cruel? Didn't he force his wife to *eat* a man who seemed to have flirted with her?"

"Yes. She was forbidden to leave the table until she was done." Rigel giggled like an idiot. He did that far too well. "And that was even *after* it was proven the poor old man was a deaf, blind, mute and couldn't *possibly* have flirted with the revolting pile of swine."

"Darn. Tough break," declared Gideon.

"For me?"

"No, for *me*. Now *both* of you are out as potential business partners. *Her*, because she'll be inconsolably distraught at losing you for a second time in one life. And *you*, on account of you having been the main course."

"Right you are, Mr. G. You are so sharp I'll have to start carrying bandages at all times," Rigel was bursting at the seams, he was so flabbergasted.

"Not so fast. I ... you ... *sizzelfacker*—" exclaimed B-T

Gideon bobbed his head. "Point well taken, but I doubt either of the Conrarf Gildefreids will be *that* charitable." He harrumphed insensitively.

"So, nameless, worthless assistantoid unit, I guess this is the part where you and I run like hell and hope to get off-world before we're so much compost."

"Right you are, sir, boss. And I *agree*."

"Wait. You ... you can't just *leave* me like this."

Gideon, who was halfway out of his chair, plopped back down. "Why is it you seem to see it that way, B-T? I've left better partners in worse lurches, often."

"You sure are a sonuvabitch, sir. Yes, you are. Are real stinker." Yeah, Rigel again, there.

"But my life is worthless. I'm toast."

113

"No. Now that's where you're *dead* wrong. If you were toast, you'd be lucky. The way I hear it, old Mr. Conrarf Gildefreid has his team of master chefs cook you from the bottom up. Any part not being actively served is left to take in the spectacle that you've become. *Damn* cruel, if you ask me, so don't. But, if you were toast, *snap*. In one big bite you'd be done suffering. Unlucky break, that's what I declare."

"Don't ask you what?" blabbered B-T.

"About how cruel this mess is, for your," Gideon gestured with a pushing-away motion, "side of the table. So, don't ask me. If you did, I'd have to be honest with you—because, seriously, B-T, you know I've always been honest with you —and that 4-1-1 would depress and upset you."

"But I am deeply depressed and upset ... already."

"Damn, I was right again. I must be part gypsy."

"You sure *are*, you gypsy king, you," lauded Rigel.

"Tell me, and, B-T, be *brutally* honest if you have to be. Which are you more? Depressed or upset?" Gideon now signaled B-T should come right at him. "I can take it."

"I ... Iyyy ... I can't say. Both, I guess ... oh, I don't know. *Sue* me."

"Come on, big guy. I'd never do that. I mean, what am I going to sue? Horsefly's colon? That's probably not going to stand up in court."

"Her *colon's* not going to stand up in court? What the devil are you going on about?" demanded a desperate man, breaking apart as he was like an iceberg on a hot day in the tropics.

"Deep breaths, dude," coached Gideon. "You're taking this kind of hard. Seriously. Think about it from my perspective. *I* always do."

"What, you're out a little money and a little time. I'm *consumed*."

"You're really fixating on *you*, B-T." Gideon rested his palm on his chest. "I gotta tell you, that hurts. Think about it like this. *I* still need to plan how to market the easiest, most lucrative product in the cosmos. You," he tossed two frustrated hands figuratively at B-T, "your worries are over before dessert hits the table. I understand it's traditionally plum pudding. I hate plums, should you need to know."

"I could run."

"Yup, that's why I hate plums."

"No, I mean I could run, flee. Yes, that's what I *will* do. I'll go straight to the spaceport and catch the first ship to anywhere."

Gideon got a you're-kidding-me-right look on his angled face.

Rigel tsk-tsked quietly.

"What?"

"Aren't you forgetting about your *wife?* If Conrarf Gildefreid can't stuff *you* down his wife's gullet, he'll opt for your lovely bride, *won't* he?"

"Move aside. I'm leaving immediately, over, under, or *through* you if necessary. Makes no difference to me." B-T vaulted from his chair and pulled the ripcord for his parachute (remember his chair was ever so high?).

It took some doing, but Gideon and Rigel were able to detain B-T, if only just.

"Easy, big guy. My middle name is Reality Check. I have to imagine you've forgotten a couple of, uh, kind of important factoids."

Still wrestling to break free, B-T huffed, "What?"

"If you stop biting my assistant's arm, I'll tell you."

B-T reluctantly did stop gnawing, but he continued to tussle, a bit.

"That's better," said a cool Gideon.

"*Yes,*" blurted our Rigel, "it most certainly is."

"If you go directly to the spaceport, and if you select the first ship departing this rock, what spaceline will it be?"

"What do you mean?"

"It's an easy question. What *company* will be ferrying you to safety?"

"All the flights are CG Space, LLP. Everyone knows that. Why?"

"And CG stands for—"

"Why Conrarf Gildefreid, every—" B-T's knees buckled, and Gideon's restraint quickly became a support.

"And, assuming the owner of the spaceline doesn't divert your flight, when you get wherever it is you are going, what is it you will need, and lots of it for hopefully a long time? Here's a hint. You will be *spending* it, but it's not *time*."

He furrowed his brow. "*Money?*"

"Bing, bing, bing, bing, bing," sang out Rigel.

"Give the man a *kewpie* doll," exclaimed Gideon.

"I don't—"

B-T fell silent when Rigel shoved an eight-inch cupie doll in his face. Yeah. He was just that good of a nameless assistant.

"Look at these items, which I submit for your consideration," Gideon stated. He handed B-T a stack of documents.

It took B-T only a few seconds to realize what he was inspecting. "These ... these are *forged* documents. You're not Trumamalt named Glebsofert. You don't even have two *heads*. These are *illegal*."

"And they're expensive," added Gideon with a wink.

"Your point, sir?" demanded the, let's face it, lifelong bureaucrat.

"So, if you want to survive," Gideon passed a hand toward the ceiling, "out there, you'll need money, money, money. You have to get some of these," he took the documents back, "or the relentless Mr. Gildefreid, and the equally relentless, and now sexually driven *Mrs*. Gildefreid, will hunt you down like a rabbit during rabbit season." Gideon aimed his imaginary shotgun right between B-T's eyes.

"But I don't *have* that kind of money," he wheezed.

"Well, assistant, tell him what I generally say, at this juncture."

"Then it's been nice knowing you, *poor person.*"

B-T looked puzzled. "Isn't that a tad bit ... er, *insensitive?*"

"No. It's downright dickish. But, hey, I'yams what I yams." To Rigel. "Lay in front of the doorway, so I might exit at a higher level."

"Yes, *sir.* My pleasure, *sir.*"

"Wait, there must be something you can do to help. You ... you two got me into this mess. The least you could do is help get me out of it."

Gideon swung an understanding arm around B-T's shoulders. "No, you see, *technically*, that's where you're wrong. The *least* I can do, which is what I'm *actually* doing, is nothing at all. I'm not lifting a finger. I'm shallow, greedy, and, if you're not making me money, you're actually invisible to me." He nodded at him with false empathy. "Now you tell me. How could I help someone who's invisible?" He thumped B-T firmly on the chest and turned to leave.

"Wait. What if I can *still* make you money?"

Gideon, who hadn't fully turned, returned a stunned look to B-T. Stunned, I tell you. "You think that's *possible?*"

B-T smiled nervously. "Sure. Hey, we were this close to making the deal of a lifetime, right? What if we, you know, did the deal?"

"I think he has an excellent point, sir," opined Rigel.

"You know, I don't pay you to think—"

"Sorr—" Rigel began to say.

"But this time I'm glad you did." He kissed Rigel full-on, on the lips. Tongue and all.

"So, what'd you think, *partner?*" gasped B-T.

Gideon put on his cunning look. "Here's the issue. Before, our partnership was based on me importing coffee, and you distributing it, under a shell corporation, of course."

"Of course," B-T agreed nervously.

"But, with you gone for good, one way or the other, that financial vehicle appears to be out the window."

"Hmm. Yes, I see where you might *think* that." B-T was sweating bullets. His tiny, last hope was easing down the drain. "Surely a man of your ... er, *experience* in such matters must know a way to, oh, how do you say it? Alter the appearance of reality?"

"You, sir, certainly are not suggesting to these ears," Gideon pointed to both of his, and both of Rigel's, "that we in any way, shape, form, or appearance of such, break the *law*, are you?"

"*Break*? That's such a judgmental, loaded term. Don't you agree?" B-T replied sheepishly.

"Normally, no. Not on your life. But, since we are betting your life, I will, in this one, solitary and single case, entertain the option."

"You see, *partner*, you can be reasonable," purred B-T.

"What did you have in mind, partner?" Gideon extended a hand, in confirmation of their deal, and their strong personal bond.

"Well, as you know, I'm in charge of keeping everything on the up and up, business wise."

"I had assumed no less."

"And, though it might come to you as a surprise, there's an endless daisy-chain of crooks, swindlers, and con men parading through my office trying to fool me into one idiotic scheme or another."

"Noooo," exhaled Gideon, again, stunned. "I mean, I watch TV, too. But I thought such dalliances were a product of pure fiction, *alone*."

"No, no, my friend. Why just yesterday a I had a pair of scammers dragged from my office and hung."

"*Hanged*," corrected Gideon.

B-T squinted. "Are you certain?"

"Oh, yeah. You hear the word enough, you remember it well."

118

"Anyway. What I have learned over the years is that there is a thing called the Nigerian Prince 419 Scam."

"*No*," Gideon hissed, absolutely incredulous.

"Yes. There are many variations upon the theme."

"Double *no*," marveled Gideon.

"Double *yes*."

"And, I'm not getting any clear picture here. How could this 419er *possibly* benefit the two of us?"

"Well, I find myself suddenly in need of a lot of money."

Gideon, not normally a religious man, crossed himself, by way of agreement.

"So, in my duties as minter, I have considerable control over vast sums of money."

"Of *course* you do. You're a *god* among men. Why shouldn't you?"

"Precisely. Anyway, if I transferred any of those funds to an account I might wish to access in the future—"

"Wait, it's coming to me. If you did that, the government, or its duly authorized agents, could track you down. You'd be eaten, and then they'd lock the pile of poop up for centuries."

"A disturbing, if accurate description," B-T responded, looking rather queasy.

Trying to appear *as* naïve and removed from the flow of logic as was possible, Gideon asked, "But where do I come into this picture, *partner*?" He came down on the word *partner* like he was Honest Abe Lincoln himself.

"Here's one possible application of the scam. What would you say if I transferred a massive amount of money into *your* bank account?"

"Huh? I'd say why the heck would someone ever do that? I mean, I think I already have too much money in there, already. Do you want to get me into trouble?"

"Nothing of the kind. *Nothing* of the kind." He patted the top of Gideon's head. "Then, after I have relocated my base of operations, in oh, say, a week, you transfer *half* of the money into my new, and more nebulous bank account."

"Half? Why only half?"

"Well, let's just say, *partner*, that would be your reward for helping out a friend, and business partner, in need."

"It would be?" he said, aghast.

"Yes, it would be."

"But, if it's illegal for you, isn't it illegal for me? I don't want any trouble."

"Yes, you don't, sir," added Rigel, most unhelpfully.

"No. Don't you see the beauty of it all?"

"I guess I don't. Darn it."

"You, sir, run a coffee importing company. Coffee, as a new brown morning fluid, comes under my sphere of influence."

"*No.*"

"Yes. And what could be *less* notable than my mintery opening up a convertible-money account with your company?"

"I ... I don't know what could be less notable. You know what?"

"What?"

"I'm glad you're on my side here. I'd hate to take you on in a real scam. You'd eat me for breakfas ... you know, I think I'll stop there. I'm seriously considering being done with insensitive."

"Flattery will get you everywhere, my friend."

"Oh, but do I know *that* for a fact," Gideon replied, albeit quietly.

CHAPTER TEN

Zebah rolled her eyes in contemptuous disgust. Then she rolled up the magazine—again. She walked over to where Gideon was sitting and struck him with all her petite might across the back of his head— again. He failed to notice—again. The poor magazine, once proud and stiff, was now more pulp than finished product.

"For the love of Mike, would you stop *looking* at that?" She whacked him again, for good measure. "This is worse than with your ten-legged-alien-porn phase. And that was oh so much worse than your previous *eight*-legged-alien-porn phase. You're out of control, Prime. You're *out* of control." She huffed away, casting the magazine onto the table—again.

Gideon felt the stings of her words as not-at-all as he did the blows with Zebah's Amateur Photography Grinders monthly periodical. He was doing the same thing, over, and over, and over—again. He would pull up his Bank of the Western Galaxy bank account, and stare lovingly, longingly, at his current balance. He would ever so gently touch the screen, but not in a harsh or forceful manner. No, there was but mutual, consensual, and respectful love and understanding between him and his current account balance.

Then, in a sudden fit of uncertainty, self-doubt, and no little jealousy, Gideon would close the browser window and reboot the entire system. That way no villain or rogue could miraculously breech Gideon's state-of-the-art security barriers. They—those evil theft-oriented people like him—would never get to his precious ... his current bank account balance. No. Never. It was his and his alo—"

There. He felt that. Something struck him across the back of his head. Odd, he reflected. It felt like ... He turned. Well, damn, if Gideon wasn't right. It was Rigel he'd been struck with. Zebah, bless her industry, was holding him by his ankles, Rigel's neck angled severely, as it rested on the hardwood floor.

"Why did you do that?" Gideon asked, coolly, and without anger.

"Because you won't stop checking that stupid, moronic, stupid account balance of ours," she howled in response.

To himself, he horrored, *Ours?* To Zebah he responded, "It can't be stupid, moronic, and stupid. It's too *large* to be any of those." He turned and pointed at the screen. "Say, would you like to take a look for yourself?"

"In an attempt to free you from your obsession, I've already *looked* at the same damn number ten times this morning."

"But, hon, the interest will kick-in at noon. Then we'll see a new, even *larger* account balance." His eyes danced, following some mesmerizing dream only he could know.

"Gideon, I know you've gone in too deep here. Seriously, when me bouncing naked on the bed doesn't distract your attention for even a microsecond, I know you're over-lusting for something that shouldn't garner such attention—again."

"That's nice, honey," he said absent of any human quality, as he turned to the computer, and entered his password—again.

"Oh no you don't." She grabbed hold of his arm and tugged at him ferociously. "You're coming to bed and making sweet love to me until the sun goes down."

"Sure, meatloaf's great for dinner."

She pulled more passionately. "I swear, Gideon, if you don't come into the bedroom right this instant, I'm dragging Rigel in and you won't see him until tomorrow afternoon."

Rigel, who had always secretly fancied Zebah, wondered if that was a valid offer. He patted his coat to see if he had pen and paper handy.

"Home by seven. Got it. Don't forget the metal wrenches."

Gideon hit the refresh icon. He was too enraptured to sign out, and back in—again.

Zebah turned to Rigel. "I hope you brought your big-boy condoms, today?"

"Gee. I ... fizz. I'll ... reffeltttt—" Small vibration began to build in Rigel's frame. He wondered if he was losing control. Suddenly, he went blind. His heart stopped beating. Rigel ignored those potential inconvenience. He'd waited so long for this tender ... well, this chance to bang Zebah until the cows came home. He had *seventy two* separate fantasies surrounding his first intimate entanglement with Zebah. Now, at the moment of truth, he was at a complete loss as to which he should cue up. Rigel began to drool. He drifted off into wondering ...

Luckily, Zebah didn't notice the saliva. She was seething at the back of Gideon's head. What, she strained to decide, could she strike him with next? A mace or battle-axe would do the trick, but both were currently out being cleaned. Rigel happened to have sufficed once. What was in between a mace and a Rigel? She drifted off into wondering ...

Gideon curtsied to his current account balance. "Would you like to dance?" he asked it.

The current account balance blushed, briefly, then the demure dear agreed, but only if it were a tango.

"Did I mention that I *invented* the tango?" teased Gideon.

The current account balance giggled playfully. Then it threw itself into a passionate embrace, all the while maintaining the requisite excellent posture.

Gideon heard *El Choclo,* building slowly in the atmosphere. He drifted off into wondering ...

PING

Gideon shook off the boisterous interruption.How rude, he reflected. Where was he? Ah yes, that first, tender kiss ...

PING. *PING*-PING.

Gideon stood, scanning to find the hateful sound, to throttle its source with ...

PING. *DING*.

Huh, he thought? Then Gideon noted the computer screen was blinking. Well, not so much the screen, but the numbers on the screen. They were flashing red. Hmm. Flashing red numbers. Was it possible, in any universe, and just and loving reality, that flashing red current account balances could represent a good turn of events?

777,928,339.01 drefs flashed hotly, brightly.

77,928,339.02 drefs quickly took those number's place.

77,928.03 derfs stared back in conjoined disbelief with Gideon.

How could ...

7.04.

"*Nooooo* ..." screamed Gideon in slow motion.

-888.05. Have a Nice Day, now flashed in yellow.

Gideon ceased to exist. He was not out-of-body, he was out-of-town in stunned, silent, disbelief. He, who was, just moments ago, fabulously wealthy, now owed the Bank of the Western Galaxy nearly a thousand derfs.

He fumbled for the pistol, kept in the desk drawer. Tears streaming down his cheeks, he pulled the trigger ...

———

Life's funny. On that topic, nothing could be more certain, more immutable.

Here is the sequence of events that Gideon was unaware of, following his departure from Minter B-T's office, a few days earlier. B-T promptly transferred 777,928,338.01 drefs into the account Gideon had set up for his sham-coffee company. Now,

777,928,338.01 drefs is a *lot* of money. That's nearly thirty seven hebbas. Yeah, we're talking big bucks, here.

Here goes the explanation. Please pay close attention. If you don't, there'll be a quiz at the end.

Dollip Vander Winkle was a second-line receptionist in accounting in B-T's mintry. He noticed that his wretched, hateful boss had shaken some stranger's hand, after having received a slip of paper from the man. Dollip had never seen B-T do anything civil or socially acceptable, so he became both suspicious and intrigued.

Shortly after his spying, Dollip observed B-T to pick up the phone and place a call. Since Dollip's second cousin, on his mother's side, worked as a third-line communications drone, down in the phone center, he quickly called Dolores. Note, if you will, she insisted her name be pronounced as, dă-low-rēs, because that was more annoying than the standard way of saying the name. Dolores was able to double-jack into the call. The moment B-T hung up, Dolores rifled Dollip a callback.

"Dollip, jew are *not* going ta believe wha I guz heard with mine *own* ears."

"Really, Dodo? What'd you hear?" He'd called her Dodo without her either noticing or caring, their entire lifetimes.

"Well, my sec'nd cousin, who works like a big shot up in da minter's office axes me to, you know, listens in on da boss's conversation."

"I ... I know, Dodo. I'm the second cousin who called you."

"Righcha are, sweetie. I'm so stupid, sometimes."

"Please go on. Please." Dollip was practiced at the extraction techniques necessary for his dingbat relative.

"So, I wantz you ta guess who B-T called? Come on, guess. It was his travel agent, Fanny Depack, you know, do one dat looks so exotic?"

"No. I do not know B-T's travel agent or what she looks like. What did he say to her?"

"Ta who?"

"Fanny Depack."

"Oh, ya know her? Anyway, he says, real deep'n serious like, 'Ms. Depack, I want immediate transportation off this wasteland. I no longer fly commercial, so please arrange for a private spaceship to take me to an unknown location. I want it at the spaceport in thirty minutes.'" Dolores coughed a few times, on account of her not being used to speaking so deep like.

"You're kidding me? Where'd he get that kind of money?"

"Are you axing me?"

"No, Dodo. Forget I said anything."

"But, sweetie, you didn't say *anything*."

"Good girl."

"Unless, a'course, ya did. I can't actually recall."

"Dodo, Dodo, focus. What else did he say?"

"No, nothing more."

"He said nothing additionally?"

"No, he said, 'No, nothing more.'"

"Why would he say that?"

"Because he didn't wanna be rude, now did he?"

"I don't know. What are you babb ... *talking* about?"

"Jew know. Afta Fanny axes him, 'Shall I make accommodations for the two of you?' meaning, a'course his *lovely* wife, he says, 'No, nothing more.'"

"Hot damn. He's leaving town without the ball and chain. This is *big*."

"He didn't say notin' about no ball and chain. Just Mrs. B-T."

"Look, Dodo, I gotta run. Thanks for your help. I owe you."

"Ya do? Dats so funny, cause I taught *I* owed *you*, since it was you doin da favor."

"Goodbye, Dodo."

"Backat—"

Dollip slammed the phone down. B-T was leaving town in a hurry, without the curse he called his wife. Not an unfamiliar tale, Dollip understood well. But the money. Where'd his paycheck-to-paycheck boss get enough money to disappear?

Dollip elected to search B-T's office. The man was gone for good, so it wasn't like anyone would care or protest. Dollip rifled the material on the desk. Nothing. He checked the drawers, including the locked ones. He pried them open with the stapler. Still nothing. Finally he rummaged through the trash. Bingo! The scrap of paper B-T took from the stranger. How could B-T be so stupid as to have simply thrown the secret, incriminating evidence away in the garbage, unshredded ? Easily. He was B-T.

Dollip studied the paper. A ten-digit number, followed by a twelve digit number. What were they? Comm-link numbers? Betting information? No, they were too long for either of those. Then it hit Dollip. It was a bank locator and account number. Come on, Dollip was thick, unskilled, and too angry to learn, sure, but he *was* a second-line receptionist in accounting. That had to count for something.

A quick computer search confirmed his suspicions. The locator number was for the Bank of the Western Galaxy. That was a financial institution of little net worth, and even fewer standards. Interestingly, the bank was historically a whorehouse. They dealt in cash exclusively, and fielded a goodly number of fetching sexual assistants, all cloned from the late interstellar porn star Dormy Doer. Yeah, the prospect of getting a piece of that action kept the Try Again Till It's Red House of Pleasure packed day and night.

Red's, as it was generally referred to, ended up having a lot of cash on hand. Their ever-increasing security and accounting staffs gradually morphed into the Bank of Try Again Till It's Red. When focus-group input was analyzed, management realized they weren't attracting any investment funds from half the planet's population. Yeah, you guessed it. Women had an aversion to putting money in a whorehouse bank. Go figure. So, the name was changed to Western Galaxy and their tasteless, vulgar logo was replaced by an alpine scene. This *will* be on the quiz, by the way. Footnotes count!

Since Dollip worked in accounting, it was easy enough for him to steal his immediate supervisor's log in IDs and security codes. Well, it was easy thirty minutes after he laced the man's tea with a powerful sedative. With that information, Dollip confirmed that The Ministry of Consumable Brown Morning Fluids had indeed made a substantial deposit in the Western Galaxy Bank, earlier that morning. It was labeled as a "convertible-money account." Convertible-money was just a nice way to say graft and corruption.

The receiving account was titled Giddy Up's Coffee Importers. Clearly that was a shell company. Dollip tapped his chin with a finger. Coffee? Where had he heard that word before? Ah, yes. He recalled something about a Norfimdian power gang engaging in *coffee* exports from some planet he couldn't quite remember the name of. Birth? Dearth? Something like that. Anyway, Dollip searched the word *coffee*. Yada, yada, yada, *brown morning beverage*, yada, yada.

Ah ha! There was the connection. Brown morning fluids. So, B-T had embezzled a vast sum of money and invested in a new product about to hit the local market—*coffee*. And, to avoid prison, or another day with his hellish spouse, B-T was leaving on a one-way ticket to the good life. That meant real trouble for Dollip. As he was the worst employee he knew of, pridefully so, surely whoever replaced B-T would fire him immediately. If the new boss was any real judge of competence, he or she would actually fire *upon* Dollip, to make certain he was no longer a member of the MCBMF team. Dollip certainly would do so, in that person's place.

Facing a lifetime of under-employment, Dollip's mind raced to come up with a scenario in which he did *not* become justifiably destitute. He chose to place a call to Greed Sweet Greed, ruler of the chocolate empire that currently ruled the planet's brown morning fluid market.

"Hello, I'd like to speak to Mr. Greed," Dollip said nervously, when someone answered the phone.

"Which Mr. Greed? We got lots of Greed here. There's Blatant Greed, our founding father. His two sons, Greed Sweet and Greed Begets, and their kids, I Am, Supreme, Tasteless, and Phil."

"There's a person named Phil Greed?"

"Yes, Begets' illegitimate son."

"Phil Greed? There's ... that's *it*? What gives?"

"If you must know, I find that remark offensive. Begets' mistress, Sally Did, simply liked the name Phil. It is a strong name, if you ask anyone other than the current Mrs. Begets Greed. What, sir, is your beef?"

"I ... I don't have any beef," stammered Dollip.

"Do you not otherwise like Philof?"

"Who's Philof? We were talking about *Phil*, as in *Philip*."

"Apparently you, in your low oxygen atmosphere, were. I was speaking of the esteemed, because he's filthy rich, *Philof*, who prefers to be called *Phil*."

"Oh wait. I see where Elvis left the building. You mean to say *Phulof* Greed, as in *full of*. Now I get it."

"No, sir, you do not. *Fulof* was disowned years ago. He currently resides on a small island where he rents mopeds by the half-day."

"Disowned? What did he do to deserve such a harsh fate?"

"You didn't hear it from me, sir, but, rumor has it he donated to a charity."

"*No*."

"Yes. One for infirm infants, or something. It's a black mark on the family, but they're dealing with it as best they can. Back, sir, to the purpose of this call."

"The shame," breathed Dollip.

"Yes. Greed only allows for spending money for intoxicants, sex, and meaningless political donations."

"As well it *should*," agreed Dollip. He truly believed that to be the case, and, if he ever became wealthy, that's how he planned to use his money, too.

"I'd like to speak to Greed Sweet Greed, please."

"No way. Not gonna happen. Never in a million life times. No. Please die so that worms may commence eating your eyes out."

"Wh … are you certain? This is important."

"You know what's important? Greed. That's all that matters on *this*, the rich side of the phone line. You are inconsequential, and should be contented with that desolate fate."

"I … er, how would you know that I'm so meaningless? Are you not presuming a lot more than the facts available to you might support?"

"No, sir. You are not a Greed. If you were, you wouldn't be calling to speak to a Greed. None of them have spoken to one another in fifty years."

"Wait, I saw a photo of Tasteless just the other day. He can't be more than twenty."

"*She* is twenty. I presume you are wondering how sexual relationships of the intimate nature are possible between spouses who do not speak to each other?"

"Yeah, kind of."

"In my orientation they said I should tell you to use your own imagination, not mine."

"Ah."

"Thank you for calling, sir, and have a greedy day."

130

"No, wait. I *must* speak to Greed Sweet Greed, it's … it's … it's a matter of," and then it hit Dollip, "of *greed.*"

"You have now captured my temporary attention. Go on, but please be advised you will be severely punished if the topic for which you are calling is not front-and-center, all-encompassingly based on greed."

"But you don't know who I am to punish me."

"Sir, all phones are equipped with a device to send an electrical shock into the ear of the user."

"No they're not."

The next sounds out of Dollip's throat were not words. They could only be characterized as cries of anguish, torment, and no little surprise.

"I stand corrected," Dollip said, with a gasp.

"You're welcome. Proceed."

"Well, I am a highly placed official in the MCBMF. I possess information that could mean the gain or loss of multiple fortunes for the House of Greed."

"Ah, you're a second-level receptionist, then."

"I … er … how could you *know* that?"

"Anyone above that pay grade is being generously supported by graft from this miserly family."

"You mean if I'd gotten that promotion to Ancillary Drone, I'd have been drinking from a fire hose of money, too?"

"Until your very head burst apart, sir. Please go on."

"Well, as to that, I'd just a soon speak privately with Mr. Greed, and not his phone handler."

"I'd like to be taller and sleeping with prettier women. But you know what, sir?"

"What?"

"I've learned to deal with my sad fate in this cruel world. Proceed."

"Well, I just found out the B-T ... er, you know him, right?"

"The B-Tster? Dude, he was here for the weekend with his wife *and* his mistress just recently. A truly awful man."

"He has a mistress?" Dollip said with envy ringing in his words.

"Lest you should become jealous, sir, don't. The term Hellbilly comes to mind, when I picture the girl."

"Anyway, B-T is in league with a representative of the Giddy Up Coffee and Frivolity Import Company. They are planning something on a vast scale. I fear it may involve the importation of this coffee stuff."

"Is it a brown morning liquid, sir?"

"It's a hard pellet that produces one under the correct conditions."

"And is this coffee product delicious, intoxicatingly so? Dare I query, sir, is it addictive—please, please, please?"

"I couldn't say. I've never even seen, let alone tasted it."

"Hmm, I may have to up the electric charge delivered to your ear, sir. Any pellet can be caused to produce a beverage. A pellet of parrot poop can. Your information hardly signals an issue to do with greed or the Greeds."

"I don't know, but I've heard there's an entire planet somewhere consumed with consuming the tea made from these plant pellets."

"A reference would be helpful."

"It's called Earth."

"Never heard of it."

"The Norfimdians have exported some, I'm told."

"Them I have heard of. I don't think any of the Greeds would like to get involved where those monsters are active."

"That is a choice for them to make, isn't it?"

"True," the impartial voice opined.

"Plus, competing with the Norfimdians may not be the smart play, in this case."

"Again, true. I will pass this information along. If it is valuable, I will be rewarded with wine, women, and wealth."

"Wait. What about me?"

"Are you, sir, a wine, a woman, or wealth?"

"Of course not."

"Then I will not be rewarded with you. I shall, in fact, insist I'm not."

"No, you mental under-performer, I meant what about my reward? *I'm* the one with the exclusive, covertly gained tip."

"No you're not. I know all about it, too."

"But you wouldn't have if you hadn't learned it from me."

"And for that I thank you."

"But I don't want your thanks. I want money, money, money."

"Then my thanks are withdrawn. Your net reward is much more valuable, sir, than money, money, sweet money, however."

"I doubt that, but go ahead. What is it?"

"What are *they*, sir. You have been schooled in two critical life lessons. First, never trust an anonymous voice at the other end of a phone call. Really, you were stupid to do so."

"So I'm beginning to understand."

"The other is to never hold the phone so closely, pressed so hard, against your ear."

"Why would I be doing that?"

"Because I just ripped you off on a vast scale."

True. Dollip pressed the phone against his head with all his will and might. He was pissed. "I've yet to learn anything from your second—"

The electric shock he received would have killed most species. Unfortunately for Dollip, it hurt in the extreme, but neither killed him nor destroyed his memory. So much for the alleged benefits of superior genetics.

Greed Sweet Greed reclined behind his insulated desk. As the years had passed, GSG had availed himself of his great wealth by eating every particle of food he could. As a result, he was, oh, let's agree on the term, *plump*. Plump, as in, say, nine hundred pounds of greasy fat draped over wholly inadequate bones, powered by completely over-matched muscles. GSG was, at that point in his sorry excuse for a life, a spherical blob. Jabba the *Hutt* would look fit and trim standing next to the recumbent GSG. And GSG was perpetually supine because he was physically unable to bend where his waist would have been, if he was thin enough to have one, which he wasn't.

Please do not fret about GSG, however. First off, he would worry over you and yours not one little bit, ever. Second, he might not have been strong enough to carry his bulk, but he was rich enough to make it a virtue. When one has enough money, the world, and all its opinions, are *flexible*, even if one's body is not. If a poor person farts in a tightly packed space, he is scowled upon and criticized. If a rich enough person issues a similar fart, it is admired, and everyone present wishes they could fart like that, too. If a person of average means takes out a loan with no intention to repay it, he goes to prison. If a very rich person does the same, he's called a clever businessman, and, again, he's admired. It is actually a wonder anyone chooses to *not* be phenomenally rich.

GSG heard a knock at his door. He *loved* it when someone knocked. He'd recently had a trapdoor installed just inside the entry to his office. It exposed a chute, that led quickly to a pit of ravenous vipers, who writhed in vast numbers between ten foot-long, electrified needles, all tipped with an irresistible poison. Most of the serpents, as an aside, were recent USC law school graduates. GSG wanted so much to pull the lever and send whoever visited to a horrendous doom. The more screams, the better was his appreciation. And who could blame him? What passes for entertainment on TV is so bad that producing your own diversion is justifiable.

"Come in, take two steps, and close your eyes," he said into his personal amplification unit. Because of his massive shroud of fat, he was incapable of taking a very deep breath. Most people had trouble hearing his spoken words without the device.

There was, if you'd heard GSG speak before, great excitement in his voice. His new trapdoor-pit was such an upgrade from his last, he could not *wait* to break it in. Previously, the spikes were mechanically slashing swords and the whole electrification system was a completely new innovation. He was titillated to an actually unhealthy level, given the sorry condition of his poor body.

Flelumf, the phone representative Dollip was so abused by, hesitated before opening the door. He was right in the middle of a fantasy in which, due to newly gained embarrassing riches, he was about to purchase two sex-slave robots and escort them to his upcoming high school reunion. He was uplifted by visions of his classmates admiring and envying him, for the first time, ever. He even fancied Courtney Vaben Fur would feel the bitter sting of regret's ... of regret's bitter *stinger*. She had told him she would go with him to the prom if he presented himself naked to the principal, Gertruda Beat-Esticles, and expressed his undying love for her. And it only counted if he did so in public, double points awarded if done during a school assembly. He did so, twice, but, after each devastating public humiliation, Courtney adamantly refused to go with Flelumf.

Slowly, with the aid of lots of alcohol and mind-altering drugs, he'd had been able to convince himself it was not all a cruel joke.

135

No. Courtney had seen him naked, and felt eternally inadequate. At least, that's what the gypsy fortune teller told him, years ago. But, that's not central to the explanation as of Gideon's disappearing bank balance, so no further discussion of that phase of Flelumf's parody of a life will be included.

"I said come in. Please hurry. I'm excited to murd ... *marvel* at you as soon as I can," screamed GSG's voice amplifier.

Flelumf entered, took one step, and stopped to bow respectfully. "My lord and better-in-every-way-it-is-possible-to-be-better-than-me, good morning."

GSG squinted. At least he seemed to be. It was hard to say if his long, deep furrows did or did not move slightly. "Do I know you?"

"Yes, my totality, you do. I am Flelumf, your loyal servant of fifteen *glorious* years."

If it was possible, the possible furrows deepened. "I don't recall a servant anything like you. You are a revolting example of someone who's not me."

"Truer words were never spoken."

"And I said *two* steps forward. You only took one."

"But, master of my molecules, that's where the trapdoor is. I can only assume that since you did not know it was me, the person you do not know, you meant to trick them into standing over the trapdoor that *I* oversaw the construction of."

"No you didn't. My assistant—oh, what's his name—did."

"Flelumf, ruler of my right to live. I am Flelumf."

"You are? Are you certain?"

"Yes, I am."

"Could you come a little closer, say one *step* closer. I have a cold in my nose, and wouldn't want for all the galaxy for you to catch it."

"Certainly, boss of bosses." He did so, quickly and without reservation. "Now, the matter I wish to discuss with you is critically important. It has to do with the security of your family's entire fortune. You see .... *eeeeee*—"

GSG's multiple video camera documented, from every imaginable angle, Flelumf descent into the Pit of Despair, as GSG had only recently re-named it. The still-technically-his-assistant screamed and flailed in a most satisfactory manner until he was lofted into the air at the end of the "ride portion of his experience." Flelumf's brief "aerial phase" was punctuated exquisitely by louder volumes, and the transition of all *words* in his cries, to those more *primal* in nature. Very nice.

The "first contact" and "warm welcome" segments of Flelumf's final service to his employer were a bit too troubling and graphically disturbing to be relayed in any detail. Suffice it to say, you must bend down now and kiss the ground, while murmuring, "I'm glad I wasn't that poor sod."

Greed Sweet Greed squirmed, for that was really all he could do independently, with joyous abandon for exactly seven point eight seconds. Then his brain involuntarily relayed the words the strange man had said, just before he plunged to GSG's viewing pleasure. Something about ... money? No fortune. Yes. "... the security of your family's entire fortune."

Oh, my. GSG had killed the messenger before he relayed his *critically important* message.

Oh well, GSG decided. There'd probably be another messenger along shortly. He'd hear that one out before pushing his big red DROP button.

The following morning, Flelumf's family was notified that he had quit his job. Since he left without the customary two-weeks notice, Flelumf's family would not be able to access GSG's embarrassingly miserly post-employment-benefits package. The family was cast into their own version of a pit of despair. Though

Flelumf himself was completely and absolutely unlamented, the loss of those benefits stung, like the sting of bitter regret.

Luckily for the pissed off, but otherwise emotionally unburdened family, Flelumf had embezzled a small fortune before he made the leap to quit his job with GSG.

The following morning, the family descended upon Probate Court. While justice wasn't swift on the planet, probate was. During the sleep-with-the-opposing-council phase of the proceedings, Mrs. Flelumf learned the contents of the recording made of her husband's last official duties with GSG. Those recordings, made for training and quality-control concerns, only, alerted her to the potential financial crisis posed by the Giddy Up Coffee and Frivolity Company's newest incursions.

Simsimus—that was Mrs. Flelumf's given name—made a few calls while waiting for the opposing council to finish with his undercover efforts. She moved a large sum of money from here to there, and another big chunk from right-over-there to just-beyond-that.

By noon, local, the entire CBMF market was in ruins. The Greeds lost every penny they'd ever possessed. Simsimus, and her pool boy Shemp, became the thirty-fifth and the one-hundred and fifty third wealthiest individuals on the planet. The Bank of the Western Galaxy closed all accounts by 12:01 pm. Hopefully you recall *Red*, of Try Again Till It's Red House of Pleasure, that became the Western Bank. Well, Red's bank was just a money-laundering front for a group of unsavory types. Yes, politicians. Anyway, Red's never actually had any of the funds they displayed for their customers' benefits. Nah, all the money was in some other, even less respectful bank with no standards at all. So, the planetary banking system collapsed like a string-puppet whose puppeteer was sliced in half with a mini-gun burst fired by an angry terminator.

The real story the reader needs to understand the background of is this. As Gideon sat there in horror and stunned disbelief, watching the first fortune he'd even owned evaporate into nothing but a small debt, there was a loud knock on his front door. The front door was actually shattered into a million toothpicks with the first "knock." The Norfimdians had come a-calling.

Now, we've all seen horror movies with a science fiction bent or premise. The monsters in all of those films are hideous, frightening at a DNA level, and are mindless, unstoppable killing machines. Here's the best description of a Norfimdian. If all those scary monsters in all those movies were standing *together* on a street corner and *one* Norfimdian was seen to be walking in their direction, the bunch of slackers'd run home to their mommies and hide under their dresses. If their mommies didn't wear clothes, they'd hide under her skin. And that's even be before the Norfimdian looked them in the eye and howled, "You *stold* from the Norfimdians. Now you will die, many many times."

That was the first thing Gideon heard bellowed from the first of *ten* Norfimdians as they charged past the now-toothpick front door.

Con-men don't live very long if they're not good at lickety-split escapes. Even the best of them will miss a "tell" or overestimate an advantage. *Never be too invested in your cleverness* is an old saying among scam artists.

Gideon and Zebah were up and running in less than a heartbeat. He even swept the computer he'd been obsessing over to the floor behind him in a vain attempt to slow the unslowable Norfimdians. The pair were at the back door faster than you could say, *I'm too young to die.* And it wasn't by chance that any place Gideon stayed had multiple exits. He was good enough to always provide for those.

As Zebah skidded around the opening to freedom, a massive paw snatched hold of her white lace half-apron. She'd been wearing a white lace half-apron because she was a true professional. Of late, she felt she might have been losing her competitive edge when it came to sexual-role playing business interactions. She knew, however, that practice, practice, practice was how one forged opportunity into guaranteed success. Anyway, Mallu, the lead Norfimdian, caught the edge of the delicate fabric. Fortunately for Zebah, her consummate-pro-level French maid's costume was *meant* to be torn to shreds. She broke free effortlessly and caught up with Gideon.

For his part, Gideon set an impressive pace. Almost certainly he was unaware that he was faster afoot than Zebah by a considerable margin. He'd opened up a bit of an inexcusable gap between the two of them by the time he was halfway to the getaway vehicle. His pitiful cries for his mommy's intercession did nothing to assure Zebah that, if he had the slightest chance, he'd abandon her like she was a Norfimdian herself. If he hadn't tripped, scraped most of the skin off the left side of his face, and then remained on his belly examining his wounds in a hubcap, we would never have know how truly selfish and inconstant he was capable of being.

As Zebah shot past him, she yelled, "Get up and hand me the keys."

He shot up quickly, began to quite literally run for his life, and he patted his left coat pocket, the one he always, always, always for security's sake kept his keys in. Knowing to always put them there assured him, in trying times such as these, that he would never have to shout after Zebah, "I don't have the keys. I left them on the kitchen table."

That's precisely what he ended up shouting.

She flew back to his side. "You always put them in your left coat pocket. Check again."

"No, I didn't. *Poor* con-men put their keys in their left coat pockets. *Rich* con-men put them on the kitchen table." He shrugged. "It's a thing."

140

She slapped his cheek, hard. "It is not. What are we going to do?"

They turned to see the patchwork of Norfimdians—seriously, that's what a group of Norfimdians is called, a *patchwork*—coming closer. Luckily for our heroes, for all their strength, bulk, and meanness, Norfimdians are as slow as the passage of time while sitting through a tax audit. But man were you in trouble when and if they got hold of you. CRASH! BAM! POW!

"There," Gideon pointed. "The bus. It's about to leave. *Run*."

They made it to the bus just as the driver began to close the doors. Gideon threw himself between the closing doors. The driver—Pather Sarsfield O'Shaugnessy, if anyone were to care, was the driver's name—relented, and didn't slow, but he did open the doors. They slipped on, shaken, but in one piece each.

"Exact *change*," growled Pather Sarsfield O'Shaugnessy. "Or there'll be red murder this day, by God. The pair of ye'll wish you'd niver been *born*, I say." He slapped maniacally on the side of his head as he spoke the language of the truly insane to them.

Did Zebah have a chance to grab her purse? Of course not. It was flee or die. Did Gideon ever in his life, carry *any* change, let alone the *exact* amount for two who would ride a bus? Let's not answer that question and pretend we did.

"As well as any flight of imagination might, if thoughts could think," replied Gideon, seamlessly. He was good. *Damn* good.

"Huh," Pather Sarsfield O'Shaugnessy barked.

"Mind the old lady with the cane," Gideon said quickly, pointing through the windshield. "Oh my. That's going to leave a bruise," he lamented, quietly.

"What old lady?" snarled the Celtic beast.

Gideon held one finger up, and counted with his lips, silently. The bus thudded lightly over something.

"That old lady," he said, lowering his finger.

141

"Exactchangeexactchangeexactchange," demanded an ever increasingly enraged Pather Sarsfield O'Shaugnessy. "Don't try to change the subject, be God, to avoidable death or professional liability, Black Michael. I'm over all of that, lad. *Over* it, I declare."

"*I* believe you," Gideon said, conspiratorially. Then he tossed his eyes in the direction of a delinquent-looking teenager with a perma-scowl, hateful tattoos, and ridiculously loud music blaring. "But *he* doesn't."

Of course, if Pather Sarsfield O'Shaugnessy had even known the topic of the discussion, he'd have forgotten it by then, seconds later. Fortunately, he hadn't clue one. That was not important. This was a matter of honor, now.

"He doesn't?" gasped the driver.

Gideon rested one hand on the wheel and pulled gently. "Only *half* on the sidewalk. Those're the rules. Sorry."

"Sure and it's not your fault, at all. Them's the rules, or so they've been tellin' me, for nigh onto forty-three years now and niver *once* an explanation."

"Good man. Now, as I was saying, he does not believe you." Gideon swung his head teenager-ward.

The driver leaned way over, glaring at the man-child. One hand slipped off the steering wheel. The bus veered into the median strip and pared off two light posts and one stop signal. He sat back upright and pulled roughly, and without the courtesy of signaling, back into traffic. "A'course he don't believe me, be God. That's my *son*."

Gideon looked back and forth, idly inspecting for family resemblance. There was precious little.

"Why *must* I assume your own loving flesh and blood wouldn't believe you. *Why* is your own child, your pride and joy, riding this bus. *If* that anemic specimen of humanity *is* the fruit of your loins, sir, well, I will feel compelled to slap you."

"Go ahead an' slap away. Him an' his ma do it all the time."

142

"I can't while you're driving this bus."

"Why not? Him an' his ma do all the time." Pather Sarsfield O'Shaugnessy spat at the base of the NO SPITTING ALLOWED sign. "Damn Wee John a'mine can't be doin' no work, an' school's way too constraining. So, he rides this bus on account of I don't charge him. Otherwise, he'd be on the streets looking for trouble."

"So, instead, he's on this bus, looking for trouble."

"Right you are, now! And, to be sure the lad's cut only two of my riders—so far." He pointed a boney finger toward Gideon, "Now, the coppers stated precisely there were no bad intentions—just a trifling misunderstanding on account of the boy's natural high spirits—and the whiskey, of course."

"How proud you mustn't be." Gideon's strategy was working. Not only was Pather Sarsfield O'Shaugnessy over halfway to the next stop, he was exceeding the speed limit with angry abandon.

"Life's the great mystery, isn't it? A constant reminder of our frailty, yet 'tis the only option open to us—that is, until the Good Lord sees fit to bid us come home."

Zebah lunged for the steering wheel. "Watch it. The ambulance doesn't stand a chance."

Pather Sarsfield O'Shaugnessy put a shoulder between Zebah and the wheel. He jerked it with a gusto and force his frail body didn't suggest was possible. Both segments of the bi-articulated bus lurched up on only the right sided wheels. Screeching and hissing, the bus eased itself over the ambulance, then plopped back to level like Pather Sarsfield O'Shaugnessy had planned it that way from the very start.

Every living soul on the bus, Gideon and Zebah included, cried out in unison, in one solid voice, and with honest conviction. "This is my stop."

Pather Sarsfield O'Shaugnessy slammed the bus to the curb, over said curb, and stopped against a large grouping of newspaper dispensers—the metal ones, not, thank God, the human kind. The mad Hibernian eased the door open and declared, "All ashore what's going ashore!" As Gideon shot past, O'Shaugnessy warned him, "And, Red Will, next time I clap eyes on ye, ye shameless trickster, it'll be exact change I'm expecting, not your impressive song and footwork."

Gideon didn't answer. The Norfimdians were still hot on his tail. Plus, if he ever boarded a bus again, and the driver turned out to be Pather Sarsfield O'Shaugnessy, Gideon would, most assuredly, walk to where he was going.

CHAPTER ELEVEN

Gideon and Zebah sat toward the back of an upscale hot dog diner. He sipped his coffee, between perky bouts of whistling. She sat quietly, as if some unseen weight pressed upon her thoughts. Gideon, naturally, ignored her possible distress. Come on, he thought. What are the chances she's mad at me? Like, totally close to zero. Certainly close enough to safely ignore. He returned to sipping and merrily whistling.

"I just can't help feeling we've forgotten something," she said, distantly.

"Whiskey or a hammer."

"No, neither of those," she replied dismissively.

"No, I was saying, the solution will be found in strong drink, or blunt trauma." He pulled a bottle of rot-gut out of one pocket, and a ball-peen hammer out from the other side. "Pick your poison."

"No. I think if I try a bit longer, I'll recall what it is that seems to be missing."

"Well, we're missing being dead. That one I can tell you for sure," he chuckled.

"No, that's not—" She drifted off.

"Well, and I know it's a sensitive subject for you, but we have been missing a lot of *sex* lately. Now, I don't blame you, even though it's entirely your fault, okay?"

"Shut up."

"We could start the healing process right here," Gideon gestured to the top of the small, unsteady bistro table."

"Shut up."

"Or, your place is always cleaner than mine," he said, gesturing off toward the women's and men's rooms, respectively.

"I'll take that hammer."

He slid it across, lustfully. "Now this does promise to break the jinx that seems to have descended upon our—"

145

Gideon was unable to finish his thought. The hammer struck him right between the eyes. Nice shooting, little lady.

"Now, I think that was uncalled for," protested Gideon, as he applied pressure to the pulsing bleed.

"You're probably right. Can you pass it back to me, please?"

He tossed it, instead, over his shoulder. "I'm closer to being in the right here. Don't you agree, Rigel?"

Silence prevailed.

"See, he agrees with me more than he agrees with you, moron," chided Zebah.

"He didn't say that in as many words, did you, fellow male pal of mine?"

Silence continued its ascent.

"Rigel *says* I'm right, Rigel *says* I'm right," taunted Zebah.

"Okay, Rige, it's her or me. Who will it be? We're transitioning into serious waters here. Will it be Team Gideon, or Team This Floozy Over Here." He pointed with absolutely no respect toward Zebah.

The waitress approached indifferently. "You ready to order yet?"

"I believe so," responded Gideon.

"Ma'am, what'll it be? The spam n'trout hash is really divine this morning."

"A bit rich for me. I think I'll have two three-minute eggs."

"How many hard-boiled eggs you want?" she replied with disinterest.

"None, but thank you."

"But you just said you wanted twenty-three minute eggs. If Barney tries to fry'em that long, they'll turn into ashes."

"Rigel," she huffed, "You order while I choose something else. This waitress seems to be off her A-game, today."

Ludlow, the unusually named waitress, turned to Gideon. "What'll it be, you poor, poor man?"

"I can't decide. Get his order and I swear I'll be ready."

There was a spell of silence.

"What *his* are you referring to? That priest over at table eight?"

"No one's ever mistaken you for a priest, have they, Rige?"

"Stop it, Gideon. You've hurt his feelings and now he's going to clam up like a big baby for way too long and make us regret the day we—"

She looked from the menu. Zebah rotated her head a full three-sixty. "I'm sorry. He must have slipped away to the restroom."

"The priest?" Ludlow queried, uncertainly.

"No. Our friend, Rigel. Shortishly tall. Thinnishly plump. Hair."

"You two came in all by yourselves, just the two a'ya." She angled her pencil toward the door.

"Are you saying Rigel isn't here, waitress?" Gideon challenged her.

"I couldn't say, boss. But you two were alone when you arrived. Honest to goodness. I know, because I see you, and I says to myself, 'These two won't leave a penny's tip. I hope there's someone else in their group, or I'm screwed.'"

"You're quite perceptive, my dear," praised Gideon.

"I worked here since the day I returned from Disneyland after I graduated high school. If I ain't learned it by now, I ain't gonna learn it."

"Where is Rigel?" demanded Zebah.

"How should I know?' protested Ludlow.

Zebah pointed to Gideon.

"How should I know?" He, for unclear reasons, pointed at Ludlow.

"Was he with us back at the hotel?" Zebah wondered out loud.

"Lord in Heaven. Kids, nowadays," exclaimed Ludlow.

Ignoring her, Gideon thought hard. "Yes. He had on that blue wool shirt he wears too often. I remember distinctly."

"Rigel doesn't *own* a blue shirt, any kind of blue shirt."

"Stop it, silly. The man's positively *obsessed* with blue shirts."

"I'll come back," announced Ludlow.

"Bring food when you do," stated a hangry Zebah.

"You got it, sweetheart."

"When was the last time you actually *saw* Rigel?" Zebah pressed.

"Well, there was ... No, that was you. I saw something under the bed, last night."

"That was dust."

"Ah. I know that yesterday he complained of something."

"He complains of something *every day*."

"True. Hmm. Well, after we escaped the Norfimdians, I remember he looked for exact change in his pockets. You remember that, right?"

"Not ... really."

"Well, oh, before we jumped on the bus, he said he'd catch a cab."

"That makes absolutely no sense. You're making that up. Stop that, immediately."

"If you insist."

"You know what? I think you and I ran from the apartment alone, just the two of us."

"Are you *suggesting* we left our dearest friend behind, at the mercy of those mindless killers?"

"No, I'm *stating* that we did."

Gideon looked stunned. Then he looked befuddled. Then he looked mildly constipated. "Oh my. We did bad."

"We most certainly did," Zebah said, gobsmacked.

"Luckily, there's no damage done we can't repair," Gideon rallied.

148

"Really?" hissed Zebah. "The clueless, inept, defenseless Rigel Rettlebutt, four days at the mercy of ruthless barbarians, monsters who eat their own body parts out of spite, is safe, sound, and not *feces* by now?"

"It *is* possible," he defended.

"It's possible you'll develop a conscience, you piece of work. But I'm not betting on it."

He shrugged. She was right.

"What are we going to do?" she asked.

"I'm thinking the blue-plate special. I loves me some fried bread."

"You pig. Our friend is probably dead, and you still want fried bread?"

"If he's dead, what's the hurry? And, I don't *want* the fried bread. I *need* something to steady my blood sugar. I *could* order oatmeal, but come on, that's so senior citizen. Plus, and I'm certain you'll agree with me on this, I think I *owe* it to the fried bread at this point."

She placed her face in her palm and shook her head in disgust. She called that her Gideon Position.

"What'll it be, kids?" asked Ludlow.

"The check," snapped Zebah. "I'm paying."

"You didn't order nothing. There's no check to pay."

"Next one's yours, Gideon," she snarled, as she slid from the booth.

They left quietly. And, as surely as rains fall from full clouds in springtime, they left no tip.

Gideon had them backtrack to the apartment they were renting when the Norfimdians attacked. For the generally circumspect Gideon, this was a rather bold move. To trifle with Norfimdians was a terminal way of behaving. It was like pulling the pin on a hand grenade, then casually playing catch with it at the beach with your loved ones. Tragedy was guaranteed, soon, and very soon. But, the pair had no other potential leads, so to ground zero they trekked.

Gideon fancied himself a master at the arts of disguise and stealth. Of course, he was competent at neither of those disciplines. But, self-delusion is a valuable trait, if you're a narcissist and lack wisdom. He stopped at a thrift shop and stole an outfit which he mistakenly thought would make him appear to the whole world to be a decrepit old lady. In fact, he looked very much like a middle-aged man dressing for Halloween, poorly. Zebah wore sunglasses.

They approached their old residence in furtive circles and angled forward movements. Neither sensed the presence of any Norfimdians. While that was nice, they also knew that to sense a Norfimdian's presence was to die horribly, so they were correspondingly not reassured. It took the better part of an hour, but, finally, they were across the street, gazing up at their second story flat. The shades were drawn, which struck them both as odd. Gideon was ever the exhibitionist, and paraded around disrobed in various levels on distasteful disregard. He maintained he *owed it to the world*. Let it be known the world was mute on that point.

"One of us'll need to shimmy up the drainpipe and sneak a look inside," stated Gideon, as he pretended to study the scene.

"Okay, you're *exactly* one, so you do it," she sniped uselessly.

"An old woman would never be able to scale a wall like that," he gestured with his cane. "It would draw attention."

"You wearing that get up already does."

"It does not."

"The bra usually goes on the inside. You're drawing stares as we speak, Idiots Incorporated."

Gideon was floored. "I'm impersonating an elderly soul who suffers slightly under the yoke of dementia. My disguise is brilliant."

"Your disguise isn't one, and I'm *not* climbing up the downspout."

"Very well. But, when this goes south, it's *all* your fault." He began to hobble comically away.

"Oh, spy master, did you bring that mini-camera?"

"Yes. It's in my handbag. Why?"

"Leave it with me. I want a picture of this, especially when you're falling off backward."

"My dear, I'm part monkey. I shan't—" Gideon silenced himself when he realized how very large an opening he'd left Zebah.

She smiled, clicked her tongue, and crossed her arms, but said not a word. She was treasuring the moment.

Against all odds and the laws of gravity, Gideon did manage to make it up to the second level. He leaned precariously to one side, craning his neck to get a look in a window. He relaxed back, shook his head, then strained again to look in the window. He remained in that awkward position for quite some time.

Out of frustration, Zebah made her way to the base of the drain pipe. "Psst," she hissed. "What's the hold up?"

Gideon ignored her.

"Gideon," she finally shouted, "what are you staring at?"

He looked down at her. "You'd better see for yourself. I ... I can't explain it in words."

"No. I told you I wasn't climbing that pipe. Now get down here and tell me what you saw."

Without responding, he leaned over and studied the apartment, again.

He was interrupted in his peeping when Zebah began to kick furiously at the base of the pipe. It was old, rickety to begin with, and in poor repair. The bottom section snapped off with her second blow.

"Stop that," he whispered loudly. "I'll fall."

"That's my hope, dope." She kicked even harder.

151

Just as the entire assembly crumbled and fell, Gideon hit the dirt, feet first.

"What?" she demanded.

"I ... I'm not really certain what I saw. I mean, I know what I saw, but, I just don't know if it's possible. What am I saying? Of course, it's impossible."

"What's *possibly* impossible," she howled.

"Come with me." Gideon trudged away, discarding his shawl and walking stick as he advanced.

"What? Are you sure this is wise? What if the Norfimdians are still up there?"

"Oh, they're up there, all right," he said with amazement obvious in his tone.

"If they're still there, why on earth are we—" she began to protest.

"You'll see, and you'll come to believe," he responded with a dismissive wave of a hand.

The apartment door was partially ajar. Gideon pushed it open, ever so gently. In spite of his best efforts, the hinges squealed like a piggy at market. But no one challenged their entry.

They arrived at the kitchen. "Take a look," Gideon said, blankly. His mind was obviously light years away.

"I'm not looking around that corner. *You* look around that corner," she challenged.

"Alright."

Gideon peered in, pulled back, and began to whimper pitifully, like a beaten, frightened hound.

"What?"

He indicated with a finger that she should take a look herself.

She held her breath and stuck as little of one eye around the corner as was possible. Zebah remained in that position quite a spell.

Then she pulled back to where Gideon stood, gobsmacked and drooling.

"My life ... my life," she tried to say. "It ... it'll never be the same."

"Of course not. How ... how could it? We're only non-human bipeds."

She sort of groaned. Then, because she really didn't believe her eyes, she stepped around the corner, to fully face the macabre display.

"Well, *hello* to you both," piped a cheer-ridden Rigel. "I was beginning to wonder if I'd ever see you again." He set down his serving trap. "Come on in and take a load off. Let me have a proper look at you."

"N ... n ... no," Zebah mumbled. "We're good. Totally good."

"Nonsense. Triple *Kill*," Rigel scolded a massive, seated Norfimdian warrior," you let the lady have your chair. Where are your manners?"

"Which lady?" triple Kill grunted unhappily. Please note. Anything a Norfimdian *says* sounds like they're unhappy. They usually are, so that assumption always works out well.

"Which lady?" chuckled Rigel. "Would you get a load of this lunkhead?" He gestured his head at Triple Kill.

"We're go ... good," repeated Zebah.

Triple Kill slapped the Norfimdian seated at the kitchen table to his right viciously in the back of the head. "You heard Rigel. Get up. Show the ladies some respect."

Lesser Evil's head snapped forward and back so forcefully it was a wonder it didn't snap off. "Alright, alright," he protested, or rather whined gratingly. "I just wanted to finish my cup."

"You can finish it standing over there, just as well," remonstrated Rigel, who was, by the way, wearing a frilly pink apron, tied in the back in an elaborate bow. Across his chest were stitched the words: Bestest Mom *Ever*.

The Norfimdians lumbered away, notably clutching their coffee cups on their saucers close to their chests, like they were carrying a tiny bird that had fallen from its nest.

"Sit," ordered Rigel. "Who wants coffee?"

All six of the Norfimdians present shot from where they stood, toward Rigel. Plaster from the ceiling cascaded down, the vibration was so great.

"If I have to tell you again, there'll be no *Parcheesi* tonight," warned a very serious Rigel. "Only twenty cups before noon. Any more and you'll never be able to take your naps."

Gideon walked over to Rigel, scratching his head, the entire time. "Ah, Rige, baby, I have to ... I don't know what I have to do. I, um ... Well, this is not one of the outcomes of us abandoning you with these mons ... *monsieurs,* that we actually envisioned."

"Really?" asked a surprised Rigel. "What seems so odd, if I may ask?"

"Yes. Yes, you may. Um, well, for one thing, you're not torn to pieces and eaten."

"He has a valid point," agreed a stunned Zebah.

"No, I'm not dismembered, thanks for noticing. And I wouldn't say you abandoned me. Time was short, we all panicked, and we were, um, *separated*."

"No, we *abandoned* you. To be perfectly honest, we forgot about you completely and totally," he confessed.

Rigel looked at him sternly. "If that's the way you care to see it, so be it."

Gideon seized Rigel by either shoulder and shook him violently. "Rigel, *WTF* is going on here? *The* most vicious, merciless race in the galaxy is sitting in our parlor sipping coffee. You should be most of the way through their *digestive tracts* by now."

"Ah, I see the problema," Rigel replied.

"You're even wearing someone else's hideous, tasteless apron. It's pink, Rigel. *Pink*," he squeaked there at the end.

"No, no. The gang," Rigel looked playfully cross at the Norfimdian death squad, "you knuckleheads, you," many of them blushed. It was hard to tell, beneath their plate-like scales, but blush they did. "The gang got this for me yesterday."

"You're their bestest mom ever?" Zebah asked hollowly.

"It's the thought that counts," Rigel responded.

"In this case, no," judged Gideon.

"The guys can't actually read. I regard this gift as one from the *heart*, not the *mind*."

"Rigel, may I get you a psychiatrist?" asked Gideon, tactfully.

"No, thank you."

"So, are you going to tell us how these ambulatory destruction devices became so, er, docile?" asked Zebah, who was, as usual, losing patience with Rigel.

"Well, do you recall what I was doing when our guests arrived, unannounced?"

"Running for your life?" responded a confused Gideon.

"No, just before that."

"Getting *ready* to run for your life?" asked Zebah.

"No, silly. I was making coffee. Gideon told me to."

"I did?" Gideon wondered. Yes, he had, come to mention it.

"Okay, sport, you were making coffee. Then?"

"Then the guys stormed into the kitchen just as I was pouring three cups, you know, to bring out for us all."

"Okay—" Gideon muttered.

"It's really kind of funny," declared Rigel.

"I doubt that, but go on," replied Gideon. He was losing patience with Rigel, as well.

"It turns out the Norfimdians had never tasted, or even smelled, brewed coffee."

"Huh? They export coffee from Earth," responded Gideon, incredulously.

"Yes. But they thought of it only as a commodity. They never sampled it."

"What kind of mons ... *monsieurs* regard coffee only as a *commodity*?" Gideon was indignant.

"Let's stay on the constructive side of the street, shall we?" requested Rigel.

"Go on," Gideon relented.

"So, smelling coffee, the boys naturally asked for a taste."

"They ... they asked?" queried Gideon.

"Yes, as politely as they knew how to at the time. Guess what?"

"I'd rather not," snapped Gideon.

"Coffee places the Norfimdians in a zen state, their happy place. If their caffeine blood levels don't drop too low, they're content to just sit around and play Parcheesi."

"Parcheesi?" questioned Gideon.

"Well, that part was my idea. But they're hooked now."

The assembled Norfimdians warriors began chanting, "Par-*chee*-si, Par-*chee*-si," over and over again.

Gideon was mystified. "So, you gave them coffee, and they didn't rip you to shreds?"

"Pretty much. But, I have to keep an eagle eye on these scamps," Rigel said, eying his murderous boys. "If they had their way, they'd drink it by the gallon."

"And that's a problem?" asked Gideon.

"Let's just say that a jumpy Norfimdian is a bad one to be around."

"That I can believe."

"And guess what else?" pressed Rigel.

"I'd rather not," snapped Gideon.

"The guys are so happy drinking coffee, they never want to waste time selling it. They're even done with the killing and the pillaging. Sure, all they want is to sit quietly and have another cup."

"And you think people will just let them?" asked Gideon.

"Would *you* try to kick them out of your coffee shop?" responded Rigel.

"Point."

"So, they said we're free to take over their export business, if we want," Rigel announced triumphantly.

"You mean like *actual* work? Show-up-on-Monday, labor-until-Friday, overtime-when-needed, and-have-to-agree-with-a-shit-for-brains-boss *work*?"

"I guess, if you put it that way."

"No thanks. I tried real work, once. I still have a foul taste in my mouth."

"That's because you ate the product at the burger place," scolded Zebah.

"Hey, it was free. What was I supposed to do?"

"Not eat it," she quipped back. "And it was only *free* if you stole it."

"You see the world in such a *limited* manner, my dear."

"Rigel," Zebah began, "have the boys learned to make their own coffee yet?"

"Not really. Their claws have the hardest time with the scoop."

"And approximately how long does it take this horde to down a full pot?"

"These goons," teased Rigel and he scolded them, "can polish one off in ten minutes if I watch them like a hawk."

"And how long after not having coffee do they revert to their, previous mood?"

"Quite quickly. A couple minutes and they're ready to do some dismembering."

Death Wielder, the youngest member of the group, turned his head, abashed.

"So, if we leave *sooner* than in a little *while*," she asked cryptically, "we'd have twelve minutes lead time to put space between someone's present mood and the one they'll soon be in?"

"I'm sorry, Zebah. What are you saying?" asked Rigel. He was so thick.

"That *ifyay eway amosvay ownay eway ightmay ivelay otay eesay anotheryay ayday,"* Zebah said, reverting to pig Latin.

"I'm sorry, are you catching a cold?" Rigel asked, a tad annoyed himself. "I'm having the *dickens* of a time understanding you."

"Rigel," Gideon said directly into his face, "run."

"Beg pa—"

"*Run,* you blithering fool," screamed Gideon, who was debating whether to abandon Rigel a second time.

Zebah pointed outwardly. "To the store to purchase more coffee. *Run.*"

That Rigel did understand. The last time he'd fully depleted the coffee supply, Viscous Menace had disemboweled the pizza-delivery man. The most disgusting part of that disaster was that everyone but Rigel agreed that guts on a pizza was the living end. Better than anchovies or gummy worms.

The three travelers were down the stairs and nearly half a mile away before they heard the first explosion. Soon after that, the distant cries of anguish were drowned out by the gunfire and the sirens. The moral of the story? There is none. Move on to the next chapter.

CHAPTER TWELVE

"I freaking hate this planet," bemoaned Gideon. "I figured we'd swoop in on this backward heap of parrot droppings, close a big deal or two, and be on our way, rich as you please. But nooo. We get jobs, we get scammed ourselves, and we end up in the cross-hairs of the most violent species in the western galaxy."

"I'm sorry. Did you say something?" asked a sweet Zebah. She'd looked up from her glossy fashion magazine, *Hunk of the Hour*, a tear of joy at the corner of her right eye.

"You got to be *kidding* me. I'm serious here," he bayed. "I hate Loser Central, and I'm out of here."

Zebah's face was pressed up against the pages, again. "That's nice, dear. There's no bread without a baker."

"I'm not certain you have her fullest attention," observed Rigel.

"Duh," Gideon snapped. He reached over and grabbed two serving trays. They were at a restaurant. He banged them together with all the gusto he could muster.

"No, not now. But you can dance with Rig ... Rig ... Rig-whatever-his-name-is, instead," she said dreamily as she flipped the page.

"I rest my case," peeped Rigel. "She can't even remember my name."

"I know, Reggie, it's incredible. You flash a muscular tush at a girl and she melts, like she's not got one just like it at home already."

"Rigel," Rigel insisted.

"Who's Rigel?"

"I am."

Gideon scowled. "Are you sure?"

"I am."

"Suit yourself, Gideon."

"No, *you're* Gideon."

"Well, of course I know that. But you just said your name was Gideon, also."

"No. I did not. You are not listening well."

"Hey, Zebah, the guy on page twenty three's coming to dinner tonight. He's a friend of mine's cousin."

She shot to her feet, stashing the magazine in her purse as she did. "We need to prepare. The place's a mess. You two are in it. We have a lot to do before seven."

"That got her attention," Gideon said to Rigel, with a wink.

"Are you still here?" scolded Zebah. "If you're not gone in five seconds, I'll disintegrate you both."

"I was kidding, sweetie. No hunk's coming to dinner. Well," he stuck out his chest. "I guess this one is."

"Which one," she asked in a near panic.

"This one." He thumbed toward himself.

"I thought you said hunk, not hack."

"As we're exchanging conversation, I want to make it official. I hate Earth and we're leaving."

"Fine. Bye. I can't. Raul Pulsadosois is coming to dinner. I have to do a bunch of Kegels first." She check her watch. "It'll be tight."

"I bet it will be," coughed up Gideon. "Seriously, Zebah, Gideon here. I was kidding. The pulse-master's not coming to dinner. I lied."

"Of course you lied. You always lie. That's why I know Raul is coming. You're lying about him not coming." She involuntarily fluttered her eyebrows. "And, of course he'll come."

"Look, whatever. But tomorrow morning, we're all getting aboard our ship and leaving this wasteland for good."

"Not too early, though," she admonished. "Raul sleeps in like a baby after a night of hot and juicy love making."

"What?" bleated Rigel. "How could you possibly know that?"

She handed him the magazine. "Pages twenty and forty seven."

"Gross," exclaimed Rigel, after taking in only page twenty. It was positively TMI.

Zebah got a dreamy look in her eyes. "Tell me about it."

"Let's get this straight, little lady," Gideon began, trying to sound credible. "First, you're going to bed with me tonight, not your delusion. Second, we're leaving earlier than I mentioned before, because you pissed me off about this Raul fellow, your imaginary friend."

"Fine," she said, paying no attention whatsoever. "As long as it's not too early. Raul likes a second helping, every morning."

"Lords of Light, Zeb, that's too descriptive even for me, and I'm a sicko," thundered Gideon.

"What. The boy likes his pancakes. Always has a second helping. He says it gives him *animal* magnetism."

"Pancakes? Give him animal magnetism? Rubbish. A spare tire, yes. Cavities from all that syrup, to be certain. But animal appeal? Please."

"Give me that back," demanded Zebah, as she seized *Hunk of the Hour* back from him. "You're crumpling Star Boy and Wonder Knockers."

"I was not. They were like that when you lent the magazine to me."

"And the ink stains on your fingers?" she asked angrily.

"They're from ... from my model ... hey, look over there," Rigel pointed up. "A flying elephant."

"Rige, you got caught red handed. Fess up. That old flying elephant line is—"

Gideon was forced to stop when a huge load of elephant poop fell from the sky and landed directly on his head.

"I tried to warn you," Rigel said apologetically. "I could tell he was flying kind of *heavy*, you know what I mean?"

"Mmm hhahamm mmmmha," Gideon said or responded, under that smelly mountain.

"Beg pardon?" stated Rigel.

Gideon drew a line across his lips with one finger. "A fire hose, please."

"Ah. Right you are."

A few minutes later, Gideon was recognizable again. He wasn't, however, approachable. "I'm going home and boiling myself," he announced with grand disgust.

"Do not leave the restroom a mess. Raul hates—"

"Enough with the Raul BS. There *is* no Raul. That testosterone-poisoned boy there," he pointed to page twenty, "is a photo-representation of every under-sexed, overly imaginative middle-aged woman's pipe dreams."

"If you say so. But, if you leave a mess, and, seriously, I don't know how you couldn't, you'll wake up some morning a eunuch." Zebah was serious.

"If you don't—" Gideon began. He stopped when someone rested a hand on his shoulder. The hand was, no big surprise, gloved.

"Please do not you jell at my dream date, my sir," said a large, deeply tanned man-child. "If you will upset 'er, it will require me twice the time to rub down her tension."

"Keep *shouting*," Zebah screamed directly into Gideon's ear.

"No, querida mia, do not you waste shouting energy. I will harvest it, in the fullness of our passion-life together."

Zebah officially melted. Yup. All there was on the floor was a puddle of Zebah, but, it should be noted, it was a *smiling* puddle.

"Who the devil are you?" demanded Gideon.

The sculpted demigod, clad only in sculpted-demigod clothing, turned to Gideon. "I yam Raul Pulsadosois, a slave of love, and a master of burning devotion. I would shake your hand, but you are not a female type."

"Oh, it would be, what, a waste of your time and otherwise cramped schedule?"

"No, you are correct. I'm completely indifferent toward my own gender."

"Have you considered taking thinking lessons? Maybe speaking-not-like-a-boob classes," Gideon twisted that verbal knife.

Raul got a distant look in his eyes. "Ah yes, the boobs—"

"How can you be here? I totally invented you not ten minutes ago?" posed Gideon

"No, you are sorry. *I* invented *you* not ten minutes ago," replied Raul. "I was talking to my cousin, the one I wrote-in as your friend, Wondinia. She spoke so highly of you, I decided to," he flurried his hands in the air, "fabricate you."

"No, no. I was the creative mind. *I* pulled *you* out of my ass. I was trying to get under my girlfriend's skin."

"Me, too."

"I resent that remark."

"Jew are welcome."

"No, I mean I take great offense at your crass remark."

"Then, should I say jew are *not* welcome?"

"No, you shouldn't say a thing. You cannot be. I lied to my girlfriend because she was not paying me the attention and respect I was due. I tricked her into acknowledging me by making up a silly story about you coming to visit."

"An' here I am." He bowed deeply.

"No. You don't seem to get it. I was a heel, a louse, a fully *inadequate* person. That said, those foibles do not somehow allow you to be created. That's absurd."

"Yes, I know I yam, are not I?"

"You know, your annoying habit of saying really stupid things is really ... what's the word? *Annoying*."

"That could possibly be so. If you would do me the favor of speaking your prior words into my thong, I would be prepared to leave."

"Whaffutuutafff?" stammered Gideon. "First, and foremost, I am not getting anywhere near your thong with my face, or any other part of me. Second—"

Raul held up his thong, his rubber flip-flop sandals.

"Ah, that type of thong," Gideon self-corrected. "So, if I repeat whatever it was I just said into your shoe, you'll leave me, forever?"

"Forever is a berry long time. Let us just agree I will go away."

Frustrated and confused, Gideon repeated his mea culpa into Raul's go-ahead.

As soon as Gideon was finished with the *fully inadequate person* part, Raul placed his sandal back on his foot.

Zebah rose and walked over to Raul. She fished in her purse and came out with a two one-hundred-dollar bills, which she handed to Raul. "Thank you, Clarence. That was perfect."

In a distinctly Australian, as opposed to the previous mixed-Latin accent, Clarence gave her a two-fingered salute. "No problem, sheila. My pleasure. If you need me again, just let my agent know."

"Such a nice young man," Zebah pined as he departed. "And such a nice butt. I could lose myself in that butt," she double-pined. It did not dawn on her what a silly remark that was.

"Er ... eh ... fufe—" Gideon vocalized.

"I called a talent agency while you were going on, yada yada yada."

He pointed both left and right, at the same time, then up. "Ebber ... glop ... huff—"

"Because I wanted to get you on a recording confessing what a dick you are, down deep where your soul would be, if you had one."

"Buppp ... nervul ... hoppy top—"

"Yes, the thong was a wonderful foil, wasn't it? The look on your face. I'm so glad Velvet was recording the entire scam."

"Velvet?" Gideon muttered.

Zebah waved to the nearby bushes. "Say hello, Velvet."

A thin woman with a humorless face stood and returned the wave. She lowered her camera as she did so.

"You ... you set me up?" remarked a stunned Gideon.

"I most certainly did. By the way, Gideon, are you familiar with the term *viral*, as it applies to video recording and the internet?"

"Not so much."

"Well, I suspect you will be soon."

"Did I mention we're leaving this stinking rock?" Gideon managed to restate, with little force, however.

"Yes, you did," Rigel affirmed quickly.

"I know *you* know. I don't know if *she* knows, you know?"

"I know," Zebah responded rather sarcastically.

"Oh."

"Look, Gid," she began, "if you want to leave, we leave. If you are aware of a better place for us to be, we'll go there. But, to me it sounds like you're whining."

"I am noooot," he whined.

"You've been fleeced, tricked, and worst of all, you haven't made the big score. You're pouting, you're petulant, and you're piqued. I'd say get over yourself, but after all these years together I know that's not possible. As you so insightfully said you're *a fully inadequate person*." She reached again into her purse. "Here, let me play that part back to you."

"You don't need to. I know I—" He was interrupted by the booming sound of his own voice decrying his personal failure. Zebah, for the record, grinned the entire time, and a good bit afterward.

"You're never going to let me forget that, are you?" he said, in an utterly defeated tone.

"Not until the heat-death of the universe, my love. So, where are we going as part of your self-deluding geographic solution to what's actually an emotional problem?"

"Er, *not* Earth?" He did frame it, for unknowable reasons, as a question.

"I'm not familiar with that system, but it's your call. Rigel and I love to travel and will be happy wherever you drag us."

"We *do*?" wheezed Rigel, who had thought he hated travel. Change of any sort was anathema to him, he'd believed. "And we *will* be?" concluded Rigel, who couldn't recall being happy in the last seventeen years, not even once.

"I say we get on the ship and engage the hevagabor drive. We'll go where fate takes us," Gideon said with modest conviction.

"No, that we will not do." Zebah was firm in her admonition. "We haven't used it since the last disastrous time, and we will not use it again. It is the very embodiment of a curse set in motion."

"But, I'm talking about just *once*. One spin of the wheel, one roll of the dice."

"Gideon, you're talking about not being able to make an adult decision. You've never been good at those," she replied. "I love you in spite of your many shortcomings. But please, don't press me on this one. No hevagabor drive. You must decide where we need to travel next."

"Well, how about that?" snapped Gideon. "I want to place my safety, and the safety of my crew, at unnecessary and excessive risk, and now *I'm* the bad guy."

"Yes, dear, you are."

"I've led my life governed by one simple principle. There *is* no simple principle. I do what I do because I do it, not because I shouldn't have done it."

"You're babbling again, sweets. Always a bad harbinger. Wrap it up," she instructed.

"Fine. Let's go. Now."

"Where to?" she challenged.

"To ... to—" inspiration struck him. "To the *ship*."

"Gideon, sorry to interrupt," apologized Rigel. "But, I believe we are on the ship."

Gideon looked around as if a blindfold had just been removed. "Hot damn. You obeyed my orders."

"If that's how you want to see it," responded a dubious Zebah.

"Alert the media and stop the presses. My substandard crew finally obeyed a direct order."

"We're here, where to now?" asked Zebah.

"I'm going to—"

Just then there was a knock at the hull. Everyone exchanged curious glances. The ship was well hidden. Who could be out there?

Gideon looked sternly at Rigel.

"No, I did not order pizza. Do *not* blame me."

"I will blame whom I *damn* well please, as long as it's not me, you understand."

The second set of knocks were firmer, more demanding.

"I'm going to answer the door," conceded Gideon.

He stepped over quickly and pressed the *Hatch Open* icon.

"Who is it, darling?" called out Zebah.

"Emph," was his response.

"Do we know an Emph?" she asked.

"Um ... er ... *hoboy*."

"Really, dear," Zebah scolded. She rose and turned to look. "Em ... er, hoboy," she reflected.

"Are you two saying a person or persons named *Emerhoboy* is calling on us?" questioned Rigel. "That a perfectly—" he rose to look for himself. "Em ... er ... hoboy."

Gideon backed toward the others. Tiny, Tony, and Big Eddie marched forward, all with sawed-off shotguns pointed at Gideon's chest.

After Gideon pressed up against Zebah's chair, and could retreat no farther, Big Eddie spoke. "Did ya miss us, dead people?"

"Are you addressing us?" asked the dimwitted Rigel. "There are no dead persons aboard this ship."

"A situation wez will soon be correcting in ar favor," Tiny responded with a mocking chuckle.

"What a surprise, guys," Gideon was finally able to muster. "You really should have called first. We could have baked something."

"Mr. Rizzo wouldn't a'wanted ya to go to no trouble," replied Tony. He cocked the hammers back on his Trudy. Trudy was the name he'd given to his weapon. He'd actually convinced the parish priest, with Trudy's help of course, to baptize her with that name.

"To what do we owe this visit, guys?" asked a consummately nervous Gideon.

"No spoilers, ya piece a garbage," responded Big Eddie, with a humorless laugh. "We're here to deliver you to Mr. Rizzo. If he decides to fill ya wit information a'fore he fills ya with lead, dat's his call. We just works here."

"Yeah," giggled Tiny imbecilically, "we just works here."

"He said that already," complained Gideon. "Do you guys even *know* when you're being annoying?"

"I'd say wez don't *care*, more dan we don't *knowz*," replied Big Eddie.

Tiny nodded toward Big Eddie. "What he said."

CHAPTER THIRTEEN

The car ride to Paramus was burdensome for our trio. Being bound and having duct tape placed over your eyes and mouth was bad enough. The fact that it was over a thousand miles distant, as the crow flies, was all the worse. But the being tossed unceremoniously into the same trunk was intolerable, and, as Gideon tried to vocalize afterward, inexcusable. But, as with all journeys, this one to came to an end, eventually.

The first thing Gideon roared when the tape was ripped—and I do mean ripped—from his lips was, "I demand to know who *peed* on my head."

"What, youz a fussy guy, or what?" mocked Big Eddie, as he dragged Gideon out.

"If it was Rigel, I'll kill him twice and burn his ashes." Gideon was a tad flustered, obviously.

"An' what if it was da bambina?" queried Tony. He was actually curious, oddly enough.

Gideon shrugged. "Maybe I'd kind of like it," he said with uncertainty. "But that's just a hypothetical, mind you," he said with ample conviction.

"A'course. Perfectly natural, says I," observed Tony.

Tiny, to whom had fallen the dubious task of frisking Zebah when she was still a zombie, said nothing. But he had *thoughts* on that topic. Oh yes he did. Worrisome thoughts, born of the many nightmares he had had since that awful day.

"Look," snapped Big Eddie, "I presently couldn't care less who violated whom. I am concerned wit cleaning ya up a bit, so as to not cause you *pre*-verts to furder upset Mr. Rizzo on acount'a your offensive scent."

With that, he dumped the three guests into the Passaic River. He'd torn the tape off their mouths, but left them blindfolded and bound. He was, you must understand, the victim of a relentlessly unsatisfactory childhood punctuated with parents who possessed zero nurturing skills, and a wholly under-funded educational system. His being a sociopath was not his fault, so don't blame him. Blame ... others.

As an aside, to those many who have not been burdened to stand near the Passaic River, it is infamous for its level of pollution. Fish hatched in the river, for example, often grow into mutated monsters that routinely attack the citizenry from Glen Rock all the way south to New Orange. The movie *Aliens* was based on an ant colony documented by scientists to have been located just outside the township of Lyndhurst, nestled on the banks of the oozing Passaic. It was into that ignoble body of fetid water that Big Eddie thrust our brave heroes. *Bad* Big Eddie. *Bad* Passaic River.

If only Big Eddie had relented to some rudimentary level of empathy or social norms, how very different our tale might have ended. But, the thing about not knowing is that you just never know.

With their hands secured behind their backs, but their mouths agape and struggling to take in life-breath, the three were set ups for fresh-water drowning. They chugged and gagged down several quarts each of Passaic River water.

It made Gideon *mad*. He cared about his body, the temple of his massive ego. To imbibe pollutants was to degrade him as a man.

It made Rigel *better*. Several of his genetic limitations, ones he'd struggled with and against all his adult life, were altered. He, for example, no longer feared snails. His right eye, which tended to stray laterally when he was fatigued, was zapped into absolute compliance with his left eye. He looked good.

It made Zebah *transform* back into a zombie. Oh my. No one saw that coming. It turned out that the basic genetic of Hephzibah, born Lena Van Dizzle, aka Glorious Gloria, aka Zebah, were fundamentally changed by the virus responsible for her zombieness.

170

Though corrected, they were not permanently modified at a DNA level, when she was cured. Bummerness.

After a sadistically acceptable period, Big Eddie instructed the others to fish the three struggling victims out of the river. He was criminally insane, but he was not stupid. He didn't want any of that swill on him or his new brown shoes. The last time he'd pulled a body from the Passaic, it ruined a new pair of shoes. His wife even made Big Eddie donate those stained shoes to charity. Big Eddie hated giving to charities almost as much as he hated his wife, which was a lot.

Tony placed one of his meat hooks around Gideon's collar, and the other over Rigel's crotch. He yanked them out, simultaneously, like they were made of tissue paper. He shook them vigorously, then dropped them like so much baggage, on the slimy bank.

Tiny. Poor, amoral, unrepentant, homicidal maniac Tiny. It fell to him to retrieve what he considered to be *da thurd turd, floatin' in da shitter*. He took hold of one of Zebah's arms, then the other elbow, and whipped her out. Her face slapped, in gooey manner, against his, and recoiled a few inches.

"I wwwove eyou," shouted, well, Argar, now, to be fully accurate. It was astonishing that this revisiting of her deteriorated physiologic state allowed for such a wide and varied speech repertoire, as compared to her first sojourn through Zombie Ville. Nice.

Tiny did several things in rapid succession. He crapped himself, then rinsed that large load down his legs by fully emptying his bladder over it. He also relapsed, fully and completely, out of what his team of psychiatrists had termed his *shallow recovery*. He groaned, mumbled, cooed like a baby, and babbled, all at once. He was a small chrysanthemum, frolicking in a meadow, with little Bambi off to the left, and Father Christmas far off to the right. And he had presents for all the boys and girls, just not for Tiny, because Tiny was a *bad boy*.

Tiny was, in an instant, so disconnected and distraught that he kept hold of Argar long enough to allow her to plant a wet, slimy, formaldehyde-scented kiss smack on his stunned and unresponsive lips. That would not, most likely, have driven him totally and irreversibly insane. No. It was the tongue Argar slipped Tiny that did *that* trick. Greasy, covered in pustules, and colder than a witch's tit in a brass bra. Yeah, it was the Frenching that catapulted Tiny into the realm of delusions, night terrors, and interminable mental anguish. Couldn't have happened to a nicer guy, by the way, karma being the bitch that she can be.

Tiny cast Argar as far from his person as he could and jumped into the murky Passaic River. He cursed his mother, yet again. On this occasion, it was for all the swimming lessons she'd forced him to endure throughout his childhood, virtually ensuring he could not voluntarily drown himself. He swam, screaming the entire time, "Don't put those gorillas so close to my wings. They'll eat *all* the pudding." He howled that phrase over and over again until he could be heard no more. And, not surprisingly, Tiny was never heard from again.

Big Eddie followed Tiny's aquatic egress as far as he could. Then he looked at Gideon, with the purest hatred in his expression. He raised his quaking shotgun and aimed it right between his eyes. "Mr. Rizzo's not going to like *dis* turn of events."

"Why are you pointing that gun at me? It's not *my* fault you threw my ex-zombie *girlfriend* into that river. It's *your* fault."

"You know wat day say? It's never da guy wit da shotgun what's at fault."

"I am unfamiliar with that expression."

"Ya ain't now." He cocked the hammers back.

"Won't Mr. Rizzo be even more upset if you blow my head off *before* he can lambaste me?"

Big Eddie's eyes rolled. Good point. Mr. R had specifically noted that the three candy asses were to be brought before him, *in one freaking piece for a change*. Big Eddie eased the hammers back and reluctantly lowered his go-to solution for all things that annoyed him, which were as numerous as the stars in the night sky, if you're wondering.

So, back into the trunk went the three candy asses. The duct tape was disintegrated by the foul humors of the Passaic River, naturally, so the short trip to Mr. Rizzo's location was less burdensome than the previous ride. Argar enjoyed herself, immensely. It was nigh onto impossible to rile a zombie.

The limo pulled up in front of Mangia o Muori, one of Mr. Rizzo's favorite dining spots. He took all his mistresses, some of his girlfriends, but none of his wives there, he loved it so dearly. Mama Bianca, the owner, had cleared the place of all other customers, naturally. When the *Don* ate, he ate alone. Less mess, less flying bullets. He sat in the far corner, with his back to the wall. Angelo Rizzo actually liked to sit in a more airy, cheery location, up front where he could see and be seen. But, he reasoned he was *supposed* to sit in the smoky corner, so he did. Noblesse oblige could be so burdensome.

The three prisoners were made slightly more presentable before they were brought before Don Rizzo. Their clothes were allowed to partially dry, and Febreze was applied to them in excess. Big Eddie and Tony, now accompanied by Luigi, in Tiny's absence, pushed and shoved Gideon and Rigel across the floor. No one touched Argar. She followed along, a few feet behind, and that was okay by the good fellas.

"Hey, hey," Gideon protested. "I can walk, you know?"

"Yeah, but harassing the soon-to-be-dead is fun. Jew should try it sometime," taunted Tony.

"When he gonna try anything, dumbo de eleph ... elep ... pachyderm? He's going to be fertilizing the Jersey shore in less dan an hour."

"Oh, yeah." He leaned into Gideon. "Sorry to be insensitive. My parole officer says it's my biggest chortcoming. I tink it da fact dat I like to kill people, but hey, you decide."

"Shut up, da lot a'ya," snarled Mr. Rizzo. Though he could barely hear them, and couldn't care less, personally, if they harassed the meat. But he was trying to impress Carlotta Russo, well, before he attempted to impress her, otherwise. She was trying out for the number-three consort position left vacant recently when Dolores DaLuca decided to take vows, rather than live in sin, as she had been for years. The sin she didn't mind. It was the hours that wore on her.

"Alphie," Carlotta asked reaching to pinch her nose, "what's dat awful smell I smell?" She was extended the liberty to call Alphonso anything she wanted, prior to sealing the consort deal. After that, Mr. Rizzo would tell her what she could call him. Yeah. He was a tough guy, but he had a reasonable side when it came to some negotiations, especially those dealing with him and sex.

"Da dame. She smells terrible. Hey, Tiny, I taught youz said she was normal again?"

Of course, there was no response. Tiny was swimming past Wallington by then, almost halfway to Rutherford.

"Ah, boss," began a circumspect Big Eddie, "Tiny ain't wit us no more. He took a dive."

"You mean he's dead?"

"No, He jumped in da Passaic and swam away for all he was woith."

"You *lie*. No sane man jumps into the Passaic." In general, that was a lead-pipe lock truth.

"Well, da broad, she kind of frenched him, den he took da splash."

"Ah. Understandable. You should'a said dat in dat first place. I might'a shot youz for lyin' like a rug, odderwise."

"Duly noted, boss."

"Can you maybe put a plastic bag over da girl?" Rizzo asked. "I'm not sure my date can take much more a'dis awful smell."

"Sorry, Mr. Rizzo. We tried. After a couple boxes, we gave up. Day all melted."

"Alphie, does dat goil have a medical conditsion?" asked a nervous Carlotta. "Cause I'm trainin' to be a cosmologist. If I got a skin conditsion, I could be let go."

"Why would a *cosmologist* need to worry about her skin, if I might be so bold as to ask?" inquired Gideon. "Students of the science of the origin and development of the universe don't need clear complexions. In fact, most don't."

Tony slammed the butt of his gun against Gideon's spine. "*Cosmetologist*, you numbskull. And tanks for makin' da boss' flossy look like a flossy."

"Alphie, did he jus call me a flossy?" Carlotta pointed at Tony.

"Yes, my dear, he did."

"What's a flossy?" she asked with a whine.

"Er, it's what day call a gradurate cosmologist, sweet cakes. Da man's payin' ya a high compliment," explained Rizzo.

"Oh, Tony," she squealed, "ya shouldn't aught'a had, Tiny."

"He's Tony, doll. How many times I gotta tell ya," said Rizzo forcefully. "He's not Tiny."

"Oh, yes, he *is*," cooed Carlotta. She waved at Tony with her little finger as she beamed an accompanying smile.

"Does she have a sister?" Gideon asked. "I'm sort of in the market again, it would seem."

Another butt to the back silenced Gideon. But he smiled. It had been worth it. A great line is a great line.

"Alphie, who's da tall dark hamsom man ya ain't introduced me to yet?" axed Carlotta. To Gideon she announced, "I'm going to be a flossy real soon."

"Don't sell yourself short, sweetheart," Gideon replied with flare, "you're way past that. You're all the way up to recycled strumpet by now, I'd wager."

Rizzo looked to Big Eddie. They shrugged at each other, neither having the foggiest notion what Gideon just said.

"All these compliments could go to a goil's head," Carlotta said, fanning herself with a champagne glass.

"If you would allow me, my dear," Rizzo said firmly, resting a hand on Carlotta's elbow. "I have a little business to conduct upon des losers. If you could powder dat cute litl' nose a yours for a few minutes, we can get back to de non-disclosure issue surrounding da position jew're aspiring to hold."

"Oh, Alphie. When youz talks about what I want to hold, my mind does all kinds a flip-flops."

"Dare goes a sweet child," he said as she left.

He turned to Gideon. Rizzo's face went from indulgent cradle-robber to demonically possessed madman in once fluid motion. Scary guy. "I imagine jew wonder why I had youz brought here."

"A mailed invitation would have been more conventional," replied Gideon. He quickly sidestepped.

Tony flew past, shotgun butt first, and splatted onto the floor. He looked up to his boss, red-faced, and grinned like an idiot.

"Well," continued Rizzo, "guess what? I'm not gonna tell ya. Jew know why I'm not going to tell ya?"

"Let me guess, let me guess," Gideon said quickly. "Is it bigger than a breadbox?"

"Is what bigger dan a breadbox?" challenged Rizzo.

"The reason you won't tell me why I'm here."

"No, poop-head. Da reason's *metaphysical*, not concrete in objective terms."

"Is it a unicorn?"

"My justification can't be a unicorn. That's an irresponsible supposition."

"But you said it was metaphysical. Unicorns are metaphysical."

"No, they're imaginary, legendary, mythical. Metaphysical is *completely* different."

"No it isn't. Unicorns are metaphysical," insisted Gideon.

"Perhaps a common misconception. But metaphysics deals with the first principles of things, including abstract concepts such as being, knowing, substance, cause, identity, time, and space. Not farcical animals."

"I'm afraid we'll simply have to agree to disagree," Gideon replied condescendingly.

Rizzo turned to Tony. "You see. *Dis* is why I hate people. Day're so inflexible when it comes to issues dat piss me off."

Tony nodded vigorously in agreement. He had no clue what Rizzo was babbling about, but he'd learned, by not dying, long ago, to agree with the lunatic.

"I will tellz ya dis much," he said to Gideon. "Jew cost me a lot'a money. Nobody costs me a lot'a money and lives to tell about it."

"So, if I promise not to tell anyone, I'm free to go?"

"Sure ting. As soon as ya dead, you're free ta go."

The hoodlums all snickered at that inbecilic remark.

"Now, my *job* applicant will be back in a jif. I need youz gone. If you'll be so kind as to cooperate, I'd really 'preciate it. Big Eddie's gonna take you out to somewhere remote and put a bullet in da back'a your heads." He turned to admonish Big Eddie. "An' when I says *a* bullet, I mean *a* bullet. Dat bloody mess you made in Hoboken last week was completely under-professional, *Edward*."

"I *said* I was sorry, boss," responded Big Eddie, as he looked to the floor.

"Ya. You *said* you was sorry, but I don't *hear* dat your sorry. A professional is a professional in all tings." He tapped the side of his head. "a'member dat, Eddie."

"Yes, Mr. Rizzo," was Eddie's school-boy response.

"Alphie," Gideon began incautiously, "where's my motivation here? If I'm a good boy, I get a bullet in the back of the head? I should think rebellion and *non*-compliance would be indicated."

"Dares where you're wrong. If ya cooperate," he placed a finger to the back of his head, "boom, Big Eddie takes ya out. If'n ya *don't* cooperate, Eddie gut-shoots ya and let's ya rot t'death, real slow like. Very painful. I advise against it."

"May I get back to you on this issue? I can see it will take some time to sort through."

"Lamentably, no. You're dead, eider way. I'll allow Big Eddie to choose. You gat dat, Big Eddie?"

"Got it, boss. I choose."

"Right. So—"

"A question, if I might," interrupted Edward. "Can I decide *one* ting for one victim, and *another* ting for anoder victim?"

"Huh?"

"Like, can I gut shoot one, but blow da head off anoder?"

"You decide," Rizzo said, irritation rising in his tone. "The sweet lady Carlotta is returning. My mind is shifting from mayhem to matters of da heart."

"Jew are such a poet, boss," complimented Luigi. "I'm misting up."

"Tanks, my friend. On a'count a dat remark, you get to shoot someone a'deze pieces a crap first."

"Gosh, Mr. Rizzo, jew're such a kind and thoughtful boss."

"Tanks. Now," he swept his arms away, "*go.*"

"If jew peoples'd be so kind, let us transfer ourselves to da door," Big Eddie said as he waved his gun in that direction.

"And please, God, will one a'you make sure da greasy one comes along nice," pleaded Tony. "I swear, if I has to touch her, you two gonna feel real pain."

"Will that pain be before we die, as we die, or after we die?" asked Gideon with a pleasant smile.

"Out, wise guy. If I has ta shoot ya in front'a one'a Mr. Rizzo's crotch monkeys, I'll get no fruit cup afta dinner."

"There's *my* motivation," returned Gideon.

Barrels pushed the two men toward to exit. Argar followed while taking in the decor.

Just as they were about to leave, four massive Norfimdian warriors came through in the opposite direction. For as mean and fearless as the mobsters were, the appearance of such bulk and malevolence stopped them dead in their tracks. Skull Crusher, Lesser Evil, and Death Wielder followed behind their leader, Triple Kill. All four were armed to the teeth, literally. Each individual tooth in their mouths had been dentally enhanced. Their incisors had retractable razor blades, their canines harbored needles that delivered the deadliest poisons, and their molars were mortar. Or wait, were the mortars molars? Never mind. The big teeth toward the back were uber-lethal. Additionally, they carried axes, swords, plasma cannons, and little happy-face stickers to place all over a victim's body, slowing them with cumulative adhesion forces. Nasty Norfimdian warriors.

As if tangoing, the gangsters backtracked one step for each the alien thugs advanced. Ba-dum-*bump*-bump-*bump*. And so it went. Soon all of Mr. Rizzo's soldiers and our heroes were pressed up against the boss' table. The Norfimdians stopped a few paces back, towering over and drooling upon the lot of them.

Mr. Rizzo, hormonal as he was just then, became, instead of cautious and deferential, haughty and derisive. "What da hell are you morons doing here?"

The Norfimdians tapped a finger to their chests. The henchmen pointed to themselves. Neither party was certain whom the *morons* he referred to were. While both were morons, in reality, Rizzo was barking at the alien mercenaries.

"Da big ones. Geez, can't you sees I'm romancing dis flossy?"

Carlotta slipped her hand on to Rizzo's crotch. She loved being complemented. She'd grown up in a family of eleven children, and her father was a bookie. The only way to be commended in her house was to catch wind of a fix being run and report it to pops before the book closed. Since Carlotta was a shy girl, she never heard of any. Hence, she hungered for positive reinforcement, the poor girl.

"You cheated us," thundered Triple Kill.

"*I* cheated *you*. *You* cheated *me*." Alphonso charged back while pointing pointedly.

"That may be *true*, but that's not how we choose to *see* it," responded a surprisingly insightful TK.

Interesting story there. Triple Kill. You'd immediately think he killed someone three times, or maybe that he'd offed three giants at once. Something along those lines. Nope. He was called Triple Kill because he disliked mouthwash. No, seriously. One of his killer liabilities was his body odor. Boy, howdy, was it ever. The second of his killing proclivities was the looks he could give. Why, he once split a boulder right in two by rendering upon the stone a particularly nasty scowl. The Febbulian scruil he'd had hold the boulder over its head fared equally poorly. His third kill was—you guessed it—his breath. If only he'd agreed with his wives and used any brand of mouthwash, well, then he'd be Double Kill, presumably. The phone books of Norfimd were *full* of Double Kill this and thats. *Boring.*

"Maybe I choose to seez you three dead," snarled Rizzo. He stood to make that threat, Carlotta's hand still affixed to his crotch. "Ah, do you mind, flossy. Later'd be betta."

She quickly relaxed her appendage. His did, likewise.

"Ah, boss, dares four a'dem. You miscounted, again. Sorry," Tony advised him as discretely as was possible in that open-forum.

"You certain 'bout dat, Tony?" Rizzo returned.

"Kind'a."

Rizzo glowered at the aliens, again. "Maybe I choose to seez you *four* dead."

"Killing us will not solve the problem," Skull Crusher said, speaking up. He was a thoughtful maniac, always trying to clear the air, if it was cloudy.

"What makes ya tink dat?" barked Rizzo.

"I believe the answer to that question is rather obvious," replied SC. "The problem of you cheating us is not dependent on *us*. It stands separate, in time and space."

"Jeez, what is it wit you guys? What planet are you from?"

SC looked to his cohort, then back to Rizzo. "Norfimd. We thought you knew that?"

"A) I was being *rhetorical;* and B) I knows ya mentioned Norfimd before. I checked Google Maps. It's just outside of Oslo, Norway. Dat makes you guys vikings. Dats why you're so bulky."

"Are you referring to *Norfund* that is just outside Oslo, Norway? We're not from there. We're from *Norfimd.*" clarified Lesser Evil. "It's just past Aldebaran, closer, in fact, to Flign."

"What, you guys some big aliens or sompin'?" scorned Rizzo.

"Yeah, pretty much," replied Triple Kill. "You knew that, right?"

"Bunch'a jolly jokers, says I. Look, paisanos, we had a deal. I sold you torrefacto coffee from Spain dat was to die for, and you sold it in Norway or Aldebaway, wherever you said," the boss was getting flustered.

Carlotta was getting bored.

Gideon was getting hopeful.

Rigel was getting curious as to whether his navel would get larger or smaller as he aged.

Argar was getting hungry.

Death Wielder was getting antsy. He had yet to find an entrée into the conversation, and he felt left out.

"Did someone say *coffee*?" It was the restaurant owner, Joey, who had the bakery out front with the heavenly cannoli. He had a tray laden with streaming hot espressos. "If you want coffee, you got coffee." He went to the Norwegians, first.

But instead of taking a cup, Triple Kill took the tray from Joey. "Thanks."

"I'll have the same," Skull Crusher said quickly.

"Me too," piped in Lesser Evil.

"Make mine a *double*, please," requested Death Wielder, who was finally glad to be able to speak publicly.

"What, you guys tink I'm *made* a'coffee?" asked Rizzo, who was just about to lose it entirely. As it turns out, the ability to lose it entirely, violently, and unpredictably is a quality that distinguishes a foot soldier from a *don*, in organized crime. Alphonso *owned* that personality flaw.

The viscous warriors who maintained they'd been wronged didn't respond. Triple Kill had shared his tray with his blood brothers, pending their trays arriving. They were seated on the floor, right where they'd stood, sipping coffee and exchanging light conversation.

"Make yourselves at home, why don't ya?" spat Rizzo.

Still, no reply, but they were already making themselves very much at home. A curious note. If a Norfimdian is ever comfortable and at ease, he or she will be staying like that a good long while. And, just you *try* and disturb them.

"Dat's it," howled Rizzo. "I want someone, preferably lots a someones, dead. Big Eddie, so help me, I want to see da bullets fly." Silly mobster. His eyes were never that good. But, in his defense, he had lost it, so ... *duck*.

Gideon saw his opening. As Big Eddie raised his shotgun, he hip bumped Argar toward the shooter.

In Argar's state, with an addled, zombified mind, she thought Big Eddie had called her, or something. Come on, you know what they say about zombie-logic. And since Big Eddie was calling her, and she was hungry, she assumed he was summoning her ... for dinner. And Big Eddie was ... *big*.

As Edward Carlsbad Star, English by heritage, with zero Italian blood in him, was taking aim at Skull Crusher, he was unfortunately too focused on *kill, kill, kill*, and not *zombie, zombie, zombie*. It was one of an endless chain of poor decisions Edward had made in his sorry excuse for a life.

Argar opened her arms ... and her mouth.

Eddie pulled the hammers back, and smiled as only a sociopath can, at times like that.

Seeing Eddie's thumb move caught Argar's fuzzy attention. A single word flashed in her muddled head: *hors d'oeuvre!*

Eddie squeezed slowly.

Argar stuffed a napkin into her lapel.

Eddie pulled the trigger. Hmm, he reflected. Why had it hurt to pull a trigger? He'd massacred *hundreds* of people with any number of weapons with all manner of triggers. He inspected the firing mechanism. His thumb was missing. Well, he could only presume it was gone. All that he saw was the cursed spawn of Satan's mouth enveloping part of his hand and all of the trigger.

Argar realized immediately that a thumb was not going to satisfy the appetite she'd worked up, being re-transformed into the walking dead, as she had so recently been subjected to. She grabbed Big, but getting smaller, Eddie's arm and began grazing on the remainder of his hand. Mmm. Hand *good*, she thought to herself, but was polite enough not to vocalize, with her mouth full, as it were.

Big Eddie screamed. Would that was all he'd have done, in retrospect. No. He elected to grab the barrel of the gun and swing the butt at Argar's head. He neglected to take into account the pain he would be experiencing, while he swung, and she munched.

The gun flew like an eagle into the sky.

Rizzo shouted, "Someone grab dat gun a'fore someone gets hurt." Wishful thinking, at best.

The shotgun turned in the air and began its downward arc. It struck Skull Crusher right in the demitasse. He SPILLED HIS LAST COFFEE, pending, of course, Joey's refill. Rage brimmed over in the Norfimdian. Kill me, fine. Kill my family, please. But spill an excellent, piping hot cup of wonder. *DIE!*

He shot to his feet, looking for the person who threw the projectile.

That's when the gun slammed against the floor and both barrels fired off with a *boom-boom*.

One bundle of buckshot went directly into Triple Kill's ample butt. That was lucky. He didn't notice. He was, after all, so enjoying his macchiato.

The other chamber headed directly toward ... *oh no* ... Big Eddie's upper right thigh. Such irony.

The pellets found their mark. Blood spewed from Big Eddie's right upper thigh. The right upper thigh of a human male, it should be recalled, is close to, well, it's close to something dear to his heart.

Argar saw Eddie's newest offering. She officially loved Big Eddie. He knew how to treat a zombie girl. She dove for his right upper thigh, and parts nearby. Her superhuman strength allowed her teeth to sink in deeply, and, more critically, widely.

Big Eddie screamed in mortal, and anatomical, terror. He began running around in futile circles, dragging Argar, bouncy, bouncy, bouncy all the way.

"Someone get dat flossy off'a Big Eddie," howled Mr. Rizzo, in an uncharacteristic effort to easy someone's pain. Really, it was his fault, that choice of words.

Carlotta, who was up until that point, confused by what she was witnessing, believed in her small and all but useless mind, she got Alphie's hint. She bit into his crotch. While she wasn't as viscous or as strong as Argar, she did have the element of surprise on her side.

Alphonso Rizzo saw his life pass before his eyes, there in Joey Corensi's Mangia o Muori restaurant, famous for its all night happy hour. He started to pull the interviewee's head away from his you-know-what, but, alas, stars danced before his eyes, and he fainted before he could. BIG mistake. Carlotta didn't *want* the job, she *needed* the position. Her father—remember, the bookie—was deeply in debt to Rizzo for a series of idiotic wagers. Carlotta hoped that by becoming Rizzo's number-three consort, she'd be able to pillow-talk him into forgiving the enormous tab. If Alphonso Rizzo had lived, and if Carlotta hadn't mauled him so badly, and if she'd been given the job, of course Alphonso Rizzo, psychopath extraordinaire, would *never* have forgiven the debt. He'd have probably had pops killed, and maybe her, too, for good measure. But, as you'll soon see, we'll never know.

Triple Kill graciously accepted and thanked Joey for the new tray of taste-treats.

Gideon made for the nearest exit.

Big Eddie stopped running in circles. He tried, instead, to climb a wall, Argar in tow.

Alphie collapsed on the table, on his back.

Carlotta—really Carlotta, what were you thinking—got the distinct impression Alphie was "diggin' dis wit a shovel," and redoubled her efforts to please a man so renowned for being hard to please.

Tony spied his paycheck, and his secret it-can-never-be lover, Alphonso Rizzo, subjected to such a ... whatever. He *flared* with jealous rage. He bounded to the table, shoved Carlotta to the floor, and began doing what he inanely thought Mr. Rizzo really liked—the chewing off of his groin. Gross. TMI. Cover the children's eyes and ears ... hell, their noses, too, while you're at it.

Luigi saw Gideon trying to slip away. Of course, he also saw Big Eddie and Alphonso having their groins chomped on. No one was chomping on his groin, he raged. Life, he assured himself, was unfair. Because of that bitter anger, Luigi decided to kill Gideon, as opposed to interfering with either comrade's good-times, especially Tony's, because, well, the man was still so fresh. Gideon tiptoed to the door, and ... click ...

Luigi pulled his hammers back. Seriously, guys. Did none of you know those are double-action triggers? You don't have to pull the darn hammers back like it was a Taylor's 1875 Army Outlaw. Stupid felons!

Gideon stopped, mid-tip toe.

Luigi pulled at the triggers, his gun poised point blank at the back of Gideon's thick skull.

Into the door Gideon was attempting to exit exploded—what, you think he wouldn't factor in at the climax—Swobo Grabski. The maniac held four bloody machetes overhead. Seriously, Swobo, four machetes? You're just doing that for effect, not lethality. One machete, sure. Two? Eh, okay. But four? You can't grip them properly. One ill-fated swing and a blade is bound to fly off harmlessly. Silly delusional psychotic.

No one, however, criticized Swobo as he charged. What with his screams, his drooling, and the fact that he'd forgotten—yet again—to wear pants that day, he was immediately labeled a Do-Not-Criticize Individual by everyone.

Luigi, stunned only for a fraction of a second, wielded his weapon to fight off Swobo. Just as he successfully pulled both triggers, Swobo chopped the barrels on half. The shotgun fired in an unpredictable direction, which also happened to be, right at Tony, the one chewing off the tender regions of his employer at the time.

Twenty yards away, the pellets dispersed just enough to only rip the scalp off of the completely bald gangster, the top of whose head was ... ah ... directed horizontally. Blood fountained all over Rizzo and cascaded to the restaurant floor. Note to the reader. There was sawdust on the floor in a stupid attempt on Joey's part to be rustic. There was not *nearly* enough, however, to lessen the slickness of the floor.

Tony clutched his wounded head, screamed, understandably, and instinctively vaulted over the table. He hit the under-sawdusted floor and slid away like it was ice. He looked exactly like he was trying to steal second base in a baseball game. He glanced up, amidst his pain, surprise, and all-encompassing misery. He saw the backside of Three Kill.

The Norfimdian pack leader was about to enjoy that first, steamiest, sip of a powerful espresso. The impact of Tony took out Triple Kills legs. He therefore poured the scalding hot coffee onto his face. He didn't like or appreciate any attempt to melt his face, so he immediately began to search for someone to kill, preferably the one actually responsible for the affront.

He fixated on, of all candidates, Rigel. Amidst the blood, the rage, and the carnage, Rigel was bent at his waist, studying his navel.

He was watching to see if it shrank or widened, as he stood there, aging. He really was a dull fellow.

Three Kill stormed at Rigel.

Rigel looked up. Rigel became frightened. Rigel started running backwards, very fast.

Luigi, who'd reloaded his damaged shotgun, stood directly behind Rigel. He was hunting for either Gideon or Swobo. He had scores to settle. There! Swobo was chasing Gideon. No way was Luigi going to let SOB 2 kill SOB 1. He would do all the SOB slaying this fine afternoon. He fired one barrel at Swobo. That's precisely when Rigel slammed into him.

Swobo, dropped all four machetes and grabbed his butt. It was suddenly on fire with pain. As he was still running, he kicked one blade into the air, and slipped on another. As he skidded across the floor, he came to a really slick section. He glanced up, and saw he was careening toward the downed Tony, still holding onto his denuded skull with all his remaining strength.

Tony chanced to see Swobo heading right for him. Although Tony couldn't be certain, he was under the clear impression Swobo's right foot was aimed at his head. He added a whimper to his screams.

The one airborne machete arced downward. Where was it heading?

Tony braced for the impending worst moment of his life.

Three Kill charged after the retreating Rigel.

Luigi, who was run over by Rigel, was unhurt. He quickly popped back onto his feet.

Mr. Rizzo groaned once last time, and died, there on his back, there on top of table six.

Three Kill collided powerfully with Luigi. They tumbled to the floor, sliding over a particularly slick section, heading for—you got it—Tony's head, just as Swobo's foot crashed into his painful wound.

The machete. Where was the darn machete?

Gideon, seeing nothing but confusion, pulled Zebah off of Big Eddie's groin. That task wasn't hard, because there was little left of Big Eddie's groin, and Argar was full, anyway. They dashed for the exit.

Rigel stepped into a corner, a huge grin on his face. He bent and snapped a glance at this navel. Had it shrunk? Please, please shrink.

Carlotta finally regained consciousness, after being so rudely tossed to the floor by Tony. She looked around, taking in the macabre scene. She smiled. A costume party! She loved those. She jumped to her feet and began doing some unidentifiable but energetic dance.

There was a pile of waste, Tony, Swobo, Luigi, and Three Kill, stacked and writhing in a disorganized manner on the blood-covered floor.

Rigel frowned. He couldn't perceive any change at all.

Carlotta switched to the cha-cha. What a freak.

Gideon was almost out the door.

Argar looked back on the room where she'd had the best time—ever.

There's the machete!

Oh my. It's heading with great force toward ... the back of Gideon's neck. It is, in fact, one centimeter away from cleaving said neck into two unequal parts.

Time slowed to a stop. The blade stopped right below Gideon's excellently styled hair.

Tony stopped twisting in agony. His trials were over.

Argar stopped mid-fond glance backward.

Rigel decided his navel would stay the same as he aged. He was unsure why he couldn't move, however.

Big Eddie regretted so many life-choices. He still, against all odds, clung to the ceiling where he'd stopped, after climbing the wall, Argar in tow.

Carlotta danced with reckless abandon, but frozen in time and space. She was also frozen in her life. No sugar daddy. No skill in dancing. No chance for boot-strapping. Zero.

Luigi was a statue, one that had just shoved Swobo's ugly mug away from his face.

Three Kill was stiff, glaring at Luigi for having thrown a head in his direction.

Three-Spot stepped over to Gideon. The angel circled him, taking in the proximity of the deadly machete to his old friend's neck. He chuckled lightly. How did Gideon seem to always end up in such messes, he wondered?

Three-Spot then approached the disgusting heap of bad boys, in their contorted, bloody, repose. Dis-gusting, he reflected.

The angel then walked over to Carlotta. More disgusting, he reflected, of her cha-cha. He straightened her legs and set her arm at her sides, as if she were at attention. Better, less nauseating.

He strode past the recently deceased Mr. Rizzo, nodding impassively at the ghost of said criminal, which stood there appearing most confused.

Next, Three-Spot stepped over to Rigel. In spite of his piety and holiness and promises, again and again, to do no mischief, the angel couldn't help himself. He created a second navel on Rigel's belly. He made one navel larger than the original, and the second a bit smaller.

Finally, he walked back over to where Gideon stood, in peril. He gently pulled Gideon out of harm's way. Then he snapped his fingers.

"I'm sorry. I'll never touch that again," shouted Gideon, as he grabbed toward the back of his head.

Rigel grinned, happy with his dual navel. He was, after all, Rigel Rettlebutt, so what else might he have done?

Argar smiled at Three-Spot. The word dessert flashed like a neon sign as his finger approached her forehead.

He touched her just before she could snap the morsel off.

She was, miraculously, Zebah again. Unfortunately, there lingered a scent that could only be characterized as atrocious.

"Three-Spot," she greeted him warmly. "When did you get here?"

"Only just now."

"Hey, I think we were about to have dinner," she looked around. "That's why we're here, right? You could join us."

"I'd be delighted."

"Only, suddenly I feel kind of full. Weird, eh?"

He patted her shoulders. "That depends on how you look at it, my dear."

"*Threester*," cried out Gideon, "How's it hanging, dude?"

"It's hanging proudly," Three-Spot replied with a wink. "Which is more than I believe can be said for the late Alphonse Rizzo, or his henchman Big Eddie,"

"The boss's dead?" asked Gideon dubiously. "A little thing like that," he snapped his fingers, "and that's all she wrote?"

Three-Spot patted his chest. "Bad ticker. Too much rich food and not enough exercise, paired, as it was, with a terrible fright."

"Oldest story in the books," agreed Gideon.

"In Heaven, we call it job security."

191

Beetlebreath burst through the door. He was beetlebreathless. "I ... I go ... got here as ... as fast as I co ... could. Am I too late?"

Tree-Spot held out his hand. "That, also, depends how you look at it."

"Three-mister," the demon responded jovially, "nice to see you, as always."

They shook, then embraced.

"You look good," remarked Three-Spot.

Beetlebreath patted down his sport coat, his really really expensive Kiton's Cashmere coat. "I try to stay in shape. Possessing burns a lot of calories, I'll have you know."

"*Possessing*," exclaimed Three-Spot. "I haven't heard about this promotion. Seriously, you and possessing? I never would have guessed it."

"I thought it'd be a breeze. But let me tell you, it's a hard job to do, day in, day out." He leaned in conspiratorially. "I was late because I'm in the middle of *such* a tough case. We're trying to possess this president guy."

"Do tell."

"There's not enough functioning brain cells up there to take ahold of." Beetlebreath pointed to his head. "Unbelievable."

"I'll bet. But, if you've transferred to Possession, what are you doing slumming here? Aren't you well past handling the late and unlamented Alphonso Rizzo?"

"Barney called in sick this decade. Some type of bad clam, we think. I got the double duty."

"Barney always was a weak link. I was surprised he had enough commitment in him to throw in with your lot, back, you know, *then*."

"Nah, he just wasn't paying attention. Someone shouted, *To battle*. He thought they yelled *To bacon*. The rest was purely accidental." It hit Beetlebreath. "Did you say 'late' in the context of Alphonso?"

192

Three-Spot nodded toward the corner. "Whose specter do you think that lost soul is?"

"Unholy crap. I gotta fix this." Beetlebreath dashed to the wandering spirit and shoved it back into the lifeless body of Mr. Rizzo. Then he blew fairy dust in one of the corpse's ears. Yes, everyone in the great beyond uses fairy dust. Go figure.

Alphonso sat up gasping. He clutched, with one hand, his chest, and with the other, what was left of his groin. He collapsed back, dead again, from the shock.

Beetlebreath blew fairy dust back in the ear, then onto Mr. Sensitive's groin.

That time, when Rizzo revivified and checked, he breathed not just again, but in relief.

"What'd you break a law of creation for?" asked Three-Spot sternly.

"Orders from the top, I mean, bottom. There's enough invested in this piece of work to warrant most anything."

"It's your funeral," disclaimed Three-Spot.

"Hey, let's go somewhere for coffee," said an exuberant Gideon.

"What's this about going for *coffee*," protested Joey. "If I got enough for all those palookas," he gestured toward the space barbarians, "I got enough for you. *Sit*."

And they did. Zebah deferred when offered a cannoli. For reasons she couldn't fathom, her stomach was churning.

"Man-o-man, here we all are again," said Gideon. "The old team's back in town."

"Yes we are," toasted Beetlebreath. "So, Three-man, what up with you? Still in Miracles and Spectacles?"

Three-Spot smiled knowingly.

"What? *Give*," demanded the demon.

"I'm vice president of the Heaven Chamber of Commerce."

"No," Beetlebreath gasped.

"Is that good?" asked Gideon.

"Good?" Beetlebreath thumped Three-Spot on the arm with the back of his hand. "It's big. Really big."

"I'm just helping out where I can."

"Blah, blah, blah, says the next Archangel Michael."

"No. What," Three-Spot asked as if uncertain, "do you think that could be in the cards?"

"In the cards, he says. In the *bag*, I say."

"Wait, won't the *present* Archangel Michael be kind of upset about that?" asked a confused Gideon.

"No way. He's in charge of the rotating position. It's kind of like the Heaven employee of the month award."

"You've *got* to be kidding," exclaimed Gideon.

"It's true," Three-Spot weighed in. "Mike gets the cushie job of administering the prize. He's the one who thought it up in the first place."

Beetlebreath elbowed his old friend. "Keeps him out of Accounting for the Dead, doesn't it?"

Three-Spot tried to cover for Mike. "I'm sure he enjoyed that challenge. But, a change is always nice."

"Wait. Accounting for the Dead? Is that like doing their taxes? Why would dead people need to pay taxes?"

"No, it's a sick joke of a job,"giggled Beetlebreath.

"Why?"

"Ask Mr. Climbing The Ladder Of Success, there." He pointed to Three-Spot.

"Well, Gideon, there's really no accounting for the dead." He said that, straight-faced, but couldn't maintain. He burst out laughing. "No ... *accounting* for the ... dead."

"I don't see how that's funny," said a rather indignant Gideon, on all of our behalves.

"Well, the there's no accounting for you either," Three-Spot laughed though his nose. Snot flew everywhere, but he didn't care.

"Oh, you two are a *riot*. Someone should call the police," snarled Gideon.

"Okay, okay. We'll behave," Three-Spot was finally able to say.

"Speak for yourself," charged Beetlebreath. "Possessor here, first class, no less."

"Exception duly noted."

"Look, I hate to be the bad guy, here—not," giggled Beetlebreath. "But I do need to get back to El Presidente. I'm the *forth* demon tasked with taking over his mind. If I don't succeed, I'll probably end up in the Little Girl Section, again. Ever since that movie, that's been the worst place to work. People call an exorcist if a child so much as *sneezes*, nowadays."

"Poor baby," snarked Three-Spot. "I'll put in a bad word for you with the administration."

Beetlebreath stood. "Promises, promises."

And he was gone.

Three-Spot checked his Timex. "I'd best be running, too. The Chamber's sponsoring a potluck tonight and I'm in charge of the keg."

"Hey, I thought you had an Apple Watch."

"*Had* being the operative word. Seriously, Gideon, you think I have the time to fiddle with that contraption. It ran backward more than it ran forward."

"You *are* immortal," he responded.

"But not immortally naïve. No, give me a good old Timex and I'll keep it running, forever."

Gideon squinted at the watch. It had a green Mickey Mouse band, with a tear at one attachment. "Hey, that was my watch. I lost it at sea when I was ten."

"Where do you think I found it?"

"We were cruising to Bermuda. The water there's like twenty thousand feet deep."

"Takes a lickin' and keeps on tickin'" Three-Spot announced proudly, holding the heirloom up.

"I want it back," Gideon pouted.

"Only if you're willing to dive for it," responded Three-Spot. "If it leaves this wrist, it's going back in the drink."

"Sore winner," groused Gideon.

They were quiet a minute.

"So, thanks for helping me not get my head chopped off," Gideon said with a silly grin.

"I'd like to say you'd have gotten out of it somehow, but you weren't. I'd also like to say no worries, but, seriously, you owe me big time. *Epic* time."

"You might be right, but I'm pretty quick, you know."

"No, I don't. I also cheated just a bit."

"A member of the Heaven Chamber of Commerce *cheating*? What is the promised land coming to?"

"Vice president, not just a member. Remember, I was put in charge of vast quantities of beer." He thumbed his chest with pride.

"Dude, a keg's maybe thirty gallons of brew. Don't inflate your responsibility."

"In Heaven, they're bottomless."

"Wow. I bet a lot of you angels are, too, after all that alcohol."

"Crass, but true. *Crass*, but true."

"So, what kind of cheat did you pull?"

"I called in a marker from Death."

"Death owed you?"

"Still does. He's only partially off the hook."

"What dirt do you have on Death, The Grim Reaper, that's so juicy?"

Three-Spot wagged his eyebrows. "Let's just say we went through training together. School was rough, and so were our down times. Death, well, he was Juricious Notabobly back then, was particularly obsessed with pollinating all the flowers in the field, if you know what I mean?"

"I do not, and I do not want to know. I'm just thankful you could help. Er, how did you help?"

"I asked Death when your number was up, back there with the bloody machete. You'll never guess the hour and the day."

"Ah, today," he turned Three-Spot's wrist so he could see his Timex, "at around three fifteen?"

"Bingo."

"So, isn't that like a major violation, punishable by being tickled with a feather until your dead?"

"Beetlebreath pushed the limits, and I push the limits. It's all about balance."

"No it's not. It's all about the boss never finding out," slammed Gideon.

"You know, you're smarter than you look. Maybe than you actually are."

Gideon stuck out his tongue.

Three-Spot nearly caught it.

"So, will," Gideon looked up, "He find out?"

"He? No, He doesn't micromanage us. We're considered autonomous immortal entities." He paused a sec. "Now, my direct supervisor, she'd open up several new orifices on my backside if she found out. She's a *stickler* for the rules."

"Would I know her?"

"Maybe. Marilyn Monroe. She was some type of actor, I'm told."

"Your direct supervisor is Norma Jeane Baker, the blonde bombshell, a mole right here?" he fingered his left cheek.

"You knew her?"

"I would have liked to know her. She died too young. And I was just a kid. And in another solar system."

"Well, it's possible that someday in the future I may be able to introduce you two."

"Really," he snapped back. "You did tell me you guys have sex up there, right?"

"And elbows and knees don't get in the way." Three-Spot's eyebrows wagged again.

"Marilyn Monroe. I'm dying to meet her."

"That *will* be an essential aspect of the hook up."

"Oh. Well, at least you're implying I'm heading to the good place."

Three-Spot wound his watch, listened to make certain it was ticking, and then adjusted his halo, which was perfectly straight to begin with.

"You clearly *implied* it was a possibility."

"Would you *look* at the time," declared Three-Spot.

"There's a non-zero chance of me making the grade, right? Toss me a bone here, old pal."

"You know what? Yes. There *is* a non-zero chance of you making it into Heaven on your first pass." Three-Spot thought that was a sufficiently bland statement and was pleased with his guile.

"My first pass? What the hell's that supposed to mean?"

"Inappropriate metaphor there, if ever I've heard one. Um, perhaps I said too much. Please let the first pass issue go."

"Not on your endless dull life, bucko." Gideon rested his chin on the backs of his hands and Cheshire grinned.

"I beg your pardon." Three-Spot was certified in both guilt-trips and righteous indignation. He was, in fact, near the tops of those classes. He once shamed Mother Teresa into admitting there was something about someone back on Earth that she didn't like. Then again, so few people actually liked Sophie Tucker's singing, that revelation wasn't so surprising.

"Not a chance, my good fellow. If you don't tell me, in full, I'm running to the nearest televangelist and mentioning it and you by *name*."

"You wouldn't."

"Three-Spot," interjected Zebah, "you realize we're talking Gideon here, right?"

"Oh." His face darkened. "You're a bad man, Gideon Prime. A very bad man."

"But I'm a man about to learn what passes and Heaven have to do with each other. Wait, do you mean like a back-stage pass? You have one, you're in?"

"No. Would you like me to explain, against all the rules and my better judgment?"

"Maybe I could just ask *Marilyn*, you know, in a seance?"

"Your soul is as black as pitch, I do declare."

"Uh huh. So, give." He waved his fingers in his direction.

"When you approach Heaven, it's kind of like a merry-go-round, you know, the really old kind."

"You're kidding. I *swear* I know an actual psychic who can put me in contact with your sup."

"I'm serious. So, this large," he spread his arms wide, "really large moving roundy-going thing is what you ride. When you get near the Pearly Gates, you lean way out and try to pull Saint Peter's beard. If you do, you're in."

"That seems rather counterintuitive."

"I don't make the rules. I simply describe them accurately."

"Sorry. Go on. What if you miss? I mean, these are mostly *old* people we're talking about, with walkers and ventilators, right?"

"No they're not on *ventilators* when the approach the gates. You're such a ninny. Where would they even plug *in* a ventilator? Those things draw real power."

"I stand corrected."

"No, people are released to a neutral form on the rounder-device."

"Neutral? Don't you mean like who they were when they were young?"

"I do not. Think about it. People who had really short arms, or were total klutzes, would never get into Heaven." Clearly Three-Spot was heating up. "Benjamin Franklin."

"What-about-Ben-Franklin?"

"Do you think *he* deserved to get into Heaven on *his* first pass?"

"I didn't know him well enough to say."

"Of course not. He died," Three-Spot fluttered his hands in the air out of frustration, "a while ago. Anyway, he was so uncoordinated, so hand-eye-challenged that, check this out, I once handed him a warm blanket on a cold day." Three-Spot crossed his arms and seethed. "The man dropped it."

"I didn—"

"The place'd be full of basketball players and skilled acrobats."

"I did not know."

"So, you ride this Hummpy-Go-Round, and reach over to yank Pete's whiskers. If you make him yelp, you're in."

"Hummpy-Go-Round?"

Fingers at his chest, he wheezed, "I wasn't consulted as to its nickname. There you have it."

"What if you miss on your first pass?"

"Not a problem. Then it's just an issue."

"What kind of issue are we looking at here?"

"The machine takes eighty-three years to complete one cycle."

"Wow. That's a long time to have to wait, don't you think?"

"The riders got on dead."

"And—"

He extended his arms. "They're still dead. It's not like there's a clock running somewhere, counting down the seconds."

"But, eighty years? Couldn't they speed it up a bit?"

He sighed and scratched behind an ear. "They tried that a while back. Didn't end well."

"How could—"

"Some of the ones who were really lame at beard-pulling got bored. They discovered that, at such high angular velocities, if they let go, they'd be thrown off, far into space."

"How far?"

His eyes bulged, and he angled his head. "Very far. One particularly plump man hit *Pluto*, back when it was still a planet."

"I can see that there might be a problem with this launching thing, but I'm only mortal. What was the problem with that on your end?"

"We had to run around, scrape them off whatever they impacted, and then put them back on the go-roundy right where they were when they assumed orbit."

"A problem becau—"—

"Well, don't you get it? In the meantime, some old person had taken their spot. We'd have to convince Mildred to let Gladys have the seahorse back and find dumb old Mildred a "better" (he inserted air quotes) seahorse so she'd give the darn thing up. Then, when we went back to check on Gladys, she'd flown off to Enceladus for a dip in the ice water."

"I'm sorry. *Enceladus*?"

"It's a moon of Saturn and that's not important."

"I imagine not."

"So, it's eighty-three years. Any shorter and we couldn't keep up with the senior citizens."

"Why not have *two* Hummpy-Go-Rounds?" He wagged his brow. "Just forty-one-and-a-half shopping years until Christmas, that way."

Three-Spot looked at him sternly. "Have you ever pitched a really good idea to a bunch of old bureaucrats, who were set in their way before the Dark Ages even *began*?"

He shrugged. "Can't say I have."

"Then never try. You will be peppered with discouraging questions, made to fill out forms longer than the list of excuses from a husband caught by his wife in bed with her grandmother." He pounded his fists in the air. "And then, *centuries* later, you'll receive notice that after careful consideration the present order is—" Three-Spot looked up to Gideon, who was staring, mouth agape. "Sorry. Got a bit carried away there, didn't I?"

"No, but I wish someone had *carried* you away. Dude, that was intense."

"My bad." He rechecked his watch, or rather Gideon's watch. "I really must be off. I have to stop at home and get the deposit on the kegs before I can pick them up."

"They don't take plastic?"

"You are out of touch. There are no credit cards in Heaven."

"Why not?"

"Well, for one thing, no one in Heaven knows how to administer a complex credit system."

Gideon furrowed his brow.

"Hint: Everyone who ran one is *not* in Heaven."

"Oh, my. Gotcha."

"And I couldn't very well bring a team of camels down here with me to rescue *your* sorry ass."

"You use *camels* as currency of the realm?"

"Do you recall me mentioning the inflexible old men running the place, the ones who get *hives* just thinking about a change in how things are done?"

"Ah."

Three-Spot stood and held out a hand. "So, until next time."

"Will there be a next—"

"Would you lighten up! I'm saying so long. Don't get all existential on me. *Sometimes* goodbye just means see-you-later."

"Got it. Bye means bye." Gideon took Three-Spots hand in both of his and held on tightly. "I'll see you ... when I see you, old friend," he said with maudlin intensity.

"You are *such* an asshole."

"Wait till they get me on the Roundy-Go-Round."

Three-Spot started to correct his phrasing, or to scold Gideon, but   instead,   he   disappeared.

EPILOGUE

Gideon sat hunched over his plates, there at a table by the back wall of Katz's Deli in Brooklyn. He would be in utter despair, lost in depression most foul, were it not for the lunch he cradled before him. He clutched, as if it were his mother's teat, in his left hand his half Katz's Tongue Sandwich. In his right hand was a worn spoon. It had seen long service in support of the second-best-to-none matzo ball soup the place was so famous for. And, just beyond the bowl was a side of square potato knish. He just had to have it, even though Libke, his waitress, had warned him he was *eating with his eyes, not his stomach* because *what man needs that much food all in one meal. Hey, tomorrow's going to be here soon enough. You want a coronary before then or what?* She meant well, but couldn't express that empathy so well.

Gideon was in a pensive mood.

Zebah sat in respectful silence. Plus she was busy. Her mouth was full of the chopped liver and onions plate, which wasn't divine because *divine* was too subtle a word to describe the rich, umami heft of the meal. Liver juice drizzle from the corners of her lips, she ate with such raptured abandon.

Rigel was picking at his bowl of meat chili—hold the pickles, please, because I'm just that retched a person—that he always found too spicy, but *nothing else on the menu looked good today,* so he ordered the chili, *again*, and regretted it, *again*. Why hadn't he selected the two knockwursts with beans, served with bread and pickles—hold the pickles, please—like he promised himself he would the next time he was dragged to Katz's? He was, as they say, so salaciously in Yiddish, a putz.

Twenty minutes later, Gideon forked into his own—*I'm not sharing, so order your own if you want one*—chocolate layer cake. Zebah felt it was time to ask. "You doing okay?"

Gideon, who had that fork poised right before his open lips, waiting in salivating wonder for his first taste of Heaven, dropped the fork to the plate with a high-pitched crash. The fork skidded off the table and onto the hasn't-been-swept-cause-the-lunch-rush-ain't-over-yet floor. Great, now he'd have to try to flag down a waitress at Katz's during the lunch rush just to ask for another fork. Then he'd have to swish it in his water glass to get the saliva, or whatever, off it before he could actually take a bite of the chocolate layer cake.

"Leave me alone," he replied grimly.

"Honey, I have. I even did that thing with the bear suit you like. But even that didn't cheer you up. Come on. Why're you so down in the dumps?"

"I don't want to talk about it."

"*Duh*. But you know you have to. You know I'll hound you until you cry uncle and tell me. So, why not cut out the pain, suffering, and the exhibition of my considerable abilities to nag you to death, and just tell me?"

"*Because*," he said too loudly, "I don't want to talk about it."

She sat back, relaxed her shoulders, and licked her lips. "Gideon, please tell-me-tell-me-tell-me. I want to you to share your emotions, like I do with my mother. In fact, let me get her on the phone. I'm sure her encouragement will—"

"It all went south," Gideon exclaimed in a huff. The mother thing. It was both extremely dirty and extremely effective. That bitch-on-wheels could drive a saint to drink poison in sixty seconds, flat.

"There, I *knew* you could," she gloated. Extending the phone toward him, she asked, "So, no mom?"

"Not in this lifetime," he swore.

205

"What specifically went south?"

"Ouch," squealed Rigel.

"What?" snapped Gideon.

"There was a piece of pickle in my chili."

"So?"

"So I bit it, because I didn't see or suspect it was there."

"And *that* hurt so much you squealed like a little girl?"

"No. That was just the first word that came to me."

"Your bowl's still pretty full. Do the galaxy a favor and sink your face under to chili's greasy scum."

Zebah slapped his shoulder. "That was mean and uncalled for."

"I only said it to him," Gideon protested as he gestured to Rigel.

"Still, it's best to *practice* civility so it's available when you're dealing with a non-Rigel individual."

"You two speak of me like I'm a laboratory rat," Rigel sulked.

"There, you see. Practice on Rigel so that *if* you were to consider being cruel to a laboratory rat, you'd be able to resist."

"I'm going out front," Rigel said with disgust. "If you want my chili, that's okay. I'm done." He'd hardly touched it, *again*.

"Yeah, yeah," dismissed Gideon. "See, I was nice as I blew him off," he said to Zebah.

"Keep working on it, dear," she encouraged. "So, things could have gone better. They could have gone worse, too."

"Yeah, the machete could have sliced and diced me."

"See, you're coming around already. And I didn't have to put mom on the line, this time."

"I loathe that woman."

"Most sane people do, but that's not the point. You're only not-human. We are *all* only not-human. We try our best, we lick our wounds, and we move on."

His eyes perked up.

"I'm not licking anything, so forget it. I'm still itching from that damn bear suit."

His eyes perked down.

"So, what's next?" She wrapped her arm around his. "You always have a plan, the next one more glorious than the last. Where to next, my captain?"

That drew out a half-smile, maybe more of a smirk. "I've always wanted to go to college."

She snapped her head back. "No, seriously, where to next?"

"What's wrong with college? Education is a blessing."

"For some, maybe. I've never liked it much."

"Let's find out if you really might. The Grand University and Baby-Sitting Rich Kids Place of Naglature is supposed to be the top school of higher learning in the sector. Let's enroll."

"College?"

"Yeah."

"No."

"Give me one good reason why we shouldn't."

"Just one?" she held up a single digit.

He reflected her solitary digit.

"Hmm, let me see. College is a place where it is said there are no rules. Experimentation, both intellectual and physical, are encouraged. It is *also* full of naïve, beautiful young women hoping to get a jump start on discovering their sexuality. Okay, there's one reason, and it's a good one. Second, it costs money, and it's impossible to scam them."

"Why do you say that?"

"You think you could pry a nickel out of an academic's fingers? Those people are pros at not actually working but using other people's money to not do so. No way. So, that's two excellent reasons." She tapped her lips. "Third. Hmm. Well, there're a lot of loose girls in heat running around in skimpy outfits."

"You mentioned that already."

"No, those were the curious young women actively exploring life. I'm taking about the sluts who have yet to flunk out."

"Ah, *that* large reservoir of fleshy indulgence."

"That one."

He kissed her forehead. "Doll, you got nothing to worry about where I'm concerned. I'm your guy, and you're my girl."

"I know I don't, because we're not getting within a light year of that place."

"Silly Zebah." He grinned broadly. "Do you think one of those nubile young goddesses would put on a bear suit for me?" He tapped her nose.

She smiled, demurely. "Where do you think *I* learned how to use one?"

AND NOW A WORD FROM YOUR AUTHOR

Who Doesn't Love Shameless
Self-Promotion?

Thank you for taking the plunge and joining in on Gideon's swindling ways. Make sure you've read *The Galaxy According to Gideon*, if you haven't already. If his character seems familiar, it is. He's Maverick, Han Solo, Indiana Jones, Ford Prefect, Deadpool, and so many other lovable scoundrels. Hopefully, there's a little Gideon Prime in you, too.

Since you're family, now, hop aboard the bandwagon. There's plenty of room. Follow me at Craig Robertson's Author's Page on Facebook. Partake of the conversation and fun. Finally, I love emails. No, I'm not that needy, I just love hearing from y'all. contact@craigarobertson.com.

A word about my past works. Along very different, yet still brilliant science fiction lines, you should check out The Ryanverse. It's a series of twenty books (so far), following the adventures of Jon Ryan, as he saves, re-saves, and re-re-saves our collective behinds. It's great fun. The saga begins with *The Forever Life*. All twenty-four books of the Ryanverse will eventually be available on Audible. *The Forever*, the first installment, starts you off already.

A final favor. Please post a review for this book, especially on Amazon. They are more precious to us authors than gold.

So, over and out ... craig

ALSO BY CRAIG ROBERTSON:

BOOKS IN THE RYANVERSE:

THE FOREVER SERIES (2016)
THE FOREVER LIFE, Book 1

THE FOREVER ENEMY, Book 2

THE FOREVER FIGHT, Book 3

THE FOREVER QUEST, Book 4

THE FOREVER ALLIANCE, Book 5

THE FOREVER PEACE, Book 6

GALAXY ON FIRE SERIES (2017)
EMBERS, Book 1

FLAMES, Book 2

FIRESTRORM, Book 3

FIRES OF HELL, Book 4

DRAGON FIRE, Book 5

ASHES, Book 6

RISE OF ANCIENT GODS SERIES (2018):
RETURN OF THE ANCIENT GODS, Book 1

RAGE OF THE ANCIENT GODS, Book 2

TORMENT OF THE ANCIENT GODS, Book 3

WRATH OF THE ANCIENT GODS, Book 4

FURY OF THE ANCIENT GODS, Book 5

FALL OF THE ANCIENT GODS, Book 6

TIME WARS LAST FOREVER SERIES (2019)

RYAN TIME, Book 1

LOST TIME, BOOK 2

NON-RYANVERSE BOOKS:

ROAD TRIPS IN SPACE SERIES (2019):

THE GALAXY ACCORDING TO GIDEON, Book 1

THE EARTH ACCORDING TO GIDEON, Book 2

STANDALONE WORKS:

THE CORPORATE VIRUS (2016)

TIME DIVING (2013)

THE INNERgLOW EFFECT (2010)

WRITE NOW! THE PRISONER OF NaNoWRiMo (2009)

ANON TIME (2009)

www.ingramcontent.com/pod-product-compliance
Lightning Source LLC
Chambersburg PA
CBHW070459260626
47161CB00004B/1371